The PORTAL

Skye Ballantyne

BALBOA.PRESS

A DIVISION OF HAY HOUSE

Balboa Press books may be ordered through booksellers or by contacting:

Balboa Press
A Division of Hay House
1663 Liberty Drive
Bloomington, IN 47403
www.balboapress.com
1 (877) 407-4847

Because of the dynamic nature of the Internet, any web addresses or links contained in this book may have changed since publication and may no longer be valid. The views expressed in this work are solely those of the author and do not necessarily reflect the views of the publisher, and the publisher hereby disclaims any responsibility for them.

The author of this book does not dispense medical advice or prescribe the use of any technique as a form of treatment for physical, emotional, or medical problems without the advice of a physician, either directly or indirectly. The intent of the author is only to offer information of a general nature to help you in your quest for emotional and spiritual well-being. In the event you use any of the information in this book for yourself, which is your constitutional right, the author and the publisher assume no responsibility for your actions.

Print information available on the last page.

ISBN: 978-1-9822-4524-5 (sc)
ISBN: 978-1-9822-4525-2 (e)

Balboa Press rev. date: 03/16/2020

Contents

Dedicated To:

Torri Duering

Thank you for supporting me and for entertaining
all my Hunter conversations.
You know him better than anyone else.

Chapter 1

The sun was shining, its warm rays hitting her skin as her footsteps landed in a rhythmic pattern. A gentle breeze wicking away the sweat that had formed on her skin as she ran. A mile down, two more to go. She nodded her head politely at the other runners on the path. There weren't many, but the ones that were there were ones she saw every day. The people she missed if she didn't see them, but didn't even know what their names were.

Finishing her run, she quickly fried up some eggs and put some bread in a toaster. She ate her eggs quickly, trying to satisfy the hole in her stomach that was beginning to eat away at her. After satisfying her hunger, she went on to do some sit-ups and resistance training.

After showering, she headed to the batting cages to get in some practice. She got so involved with the 'thwacking' sound that the ball meeting the bat caused that she didn't even realize a man in the distance, staring at her. She never even felt the danger she was in.

After giving herself some time to rest and relax, she headed out for her afternoon run. She had it timed perfectly so that she would be home just as her father came home and together, they would make dinner, causing the house to fill up with tantalizing smells as her mother walked through the door.

She slipped out the door and ran toward the running trail,

just minutes away from her house. It was a five mile loop, and the perfect destination for a warm, afternoon run. All along the trail there were trees, creating the perfect amount of shade in order to keep from getting overheated. It also ran right by a small little stream that gurgled happily for most of the year, only freezing over during the coldest part of the winter. The grass was lush and green. Occasionally, she would choose to take a break from her run, or do an extra loop, just so she could lay on the grass and allow her mind to drift off. She often found, lying there, that her dreams were all the same, the visions of another world, but a world she felt she belonged in more than this one. She loved those visions, she loved to lay there on the grass. However, today, she was too caught up in running to even think about her other world.

She was too focused on her breathing, concentrating on her lungs expanding and deflating. She kept her breath in a nice steady rhythm even as her heart rate accelerated and she picked up the pace. She heard the sound of her sneakers as they hit the ground, each crunch of ground sent her into a meditative state, rendering her fully present and alive, while at the same time, providing an escape to some magnificent, internal realm. It was a state only a runner could understand, but it was highly addictive. It was that state, that experience which caused her to run twice, sometimes three times a day.

As she ran she noticed a vague uneasiness begin to creep into her conscious, erasing her self-created bliss. She glanced around nervously. The trail was empty save for a rather large man jogging along behind her. She shook her head, she must be imagining things. She tried to shake the unease and get back into her meditative state, and just continue her run, but it was no use. She couldn't get her mind to leave the man following behind her on the jogging trail.

'Come on,' she berated herself, 'Other people use the trail for running too. It's not mine. He's allowed to run too.'

She glanced behind her, just to confirm to herself that she was, in fact, being paranoid. That's when she noticed that he was much closer than he had been when she had looked back before. His form and breathing were irregular, she noticed. He must not run regularly. He was also wearing the totally wrong outfit and shoes for such an endeavor. Just as she began to process this information, a strong, calloused hand clapped over her mouth.

He dragged her swiftly towards a big white van that was waiting nearby on one of the trail's turnoffs. Suddenly, the ground fell away beneath her feet as the man hauled her into his arms and tossed her unceremoniously into the back of the van. It all happened so fast that she hardly had time to think, let alone try to scream.

Saralee moved toward the door, trying to find a way out. Peering out the window, she glimpsed the mountainside, thick with trees and little clearings for campsites. She tugged at the door. If she could just get it open, she could get into the trees and he would never be able to find her. It didn't budge. She tried again. Nothing. It must be locked. She searched for the way to unlock it, but it was too far down to be able to reach in and unlock it with her fingers.

The van continued onwards and upwards as Saralee continued her search. They went deep into the forest. As they got deeper and deeper inside, Saralee began to get an uneasy feeling in the pit of her stomach, and her parent's voices began playing in her head. As a child she hadn't been allowed to venture into the woods. Her parents told her to stay away, telling of the nightmares that came from the forest. As she remembered those stories, a heavy dread settled deep in her stomach.

The smooth, paved roads gave way to the unpaved, rocky trails of the mountainous forest, causing Saralee to be tossed about like a rag doll. Giving up on trying to get out of the van while it was moving, she turned her attention to try to catch a glimpse of her captor, but was unable to do so. The little window that connected the front to the back was tinted in such a way to make figuring out any features nearly impossible. She sighed. By the time the van came to a stop at an old, run-down cabin, she was sore and bruised.

The place wasn't much to look at. It was dark and dusty. The roof was falling down in places and the walls were crumbling down around the place. It was in sad shape, and looked about ready to give up and topple completely to the ground, giving up the fight it had been losing for too long.

A tall, towering figure with dark, curly black beard and hair to match it, opened the door. Instinctively she shrank back into the van. Suddenly, the large man was lifting her up with that disconcerting strength she remembered, as if she weighed absolutely nothing. The bearded man propelled her forward.

The door seemed to be the only sturdy part of the cabin, standing straight in its frame with a strong metal lock sealing it closed. It was almost comical compared to the rest of the broken walls that surrounded it. The other man came up behind them and unlocked the door as though there was nothing strange about such a sturdy door on such dismal walls.

The cabin looked even worse from the inside, if that was possible. There was dirt everywhere, evidence of the surrounding forest beginning to claim the land back. They marched her right back to the back of the cabin and shoved her into a small room that was scarcely bigger than a closet and had only one small window, whose panes were so dirty that they barely let in any light. In fact, it was almost completely dark.

They slammed the door behind her and simply left, not caring that they had probably broken her leg with their rough treatment.

After moments of silence, she heard sounds coming from the other room. She pushed herself onto her hands and knees and slid across the room to where she could hear better. She was able to discern voices.

"Now what do we do with her?" asked a young sounding male voice, a voice that she assumed came from the man who had pushed her into her unconventional prison.

"We wait until we get our orders before we do anything," a deep voice boomed.

'*That must be the bearded man,*' Saralee decided.

"When will that be?"

"Whenever our boss decides to call."

"But…"

"No 'buts', now be quiet," the deep voice growled.

Silence encased the cabin once again. Exhausted and with nothing else to do, Saralee managed to drift off to sleep, despite the pain in her leg.

Gradually, she awakened and became aware of how incredibly cold she was. The sound of a TV filtered into the room, but the walls muffled the sounds just enough that she couldn't make out what show was playing. As she lay there, her stomach growled, reminding her that she hadn't eaten since lunch.

'How long had that been? What time is it? What day is it?' she thought to herself.

As her stomach growled again she started to bang on the door, hoping she could remind them that she had basic human needs.

"What do you want?" a voice growled.

Saralee recognized the booming voice from the previous conversation, whenever that had been.

The door opened abruptly. A stocky figure stood in the doorway, the smell of cheap beer wafting off of him. Food particles clung to his beard. His voice was low and gravely, like he'd smoked too many cigarettes in his life and now he didn't have the ability to talk like a normal person. His brown eyes seemed to pierce into her, making her breath catch in her throat, choking off any words she might have said. As those sharp eyes pierced into her, she reminded herself that she had brought attention to herself and at the same time, her survival instincts kicked in. She had to try. Suddenly worried about making him mad, and trying not to make the situation worse, she haltingly voiced her request.

"C...can I have something to eat?" she hated the way her voice shook as she spoke.

"Why?"

"I...I haven't eaten for a long time. I'm getting hungry…" she felt the blood beating its dance of fear in her ears and her own voice sounded foreign to her.

"You'll get fed when I decide to feed you," with that he slammed the door, narrowly missing her nose.

Using the door handle, she pulled herself to her feet and tried to walk to the window, but as soon as she put the slightest bit of weight on her left leg, a fiery pain shot up her leg. She crumpled in a heap and lost consciousness before she hit the floor.

Chapter 2

It had been a bad day for Jesse and Jordan. Their parents had come home drunk after gambling all afternoon. Jesse was called downstairs almost immediately. Jesse looked over at her twin brother with fear in her sky blue eyes. Jordan noticed how his sister's shoulders slumped as she walked downstairs, her curly blonde hair grazing her shoulders. He despised his parents, despised the way that they could do what they were doing and get away with it.

Today, while his sister was downstairs, dealing with who knew what, he held his breath, waiting to be called downstairs as well. He squared his shoulders, waiting to see what his parents' wrath had in store for him. He waited and waited, but nothing happened. Today was the day that their parents had seemed to forget about him.

The late afternoon light had turned to dark evening light by the time Jesse came back upstairs to their room. It wasn't much of a place, just two beds and a dresser that the two of them had to share. They had no decorations, nothing to make the room say anything about the two people who lived there. It was just a small, forgotten room at the end of the hall. There was barely enough to squeeze the furniture they had inside.

Jesse walked slowly into the room. Her hair was a mess and her clothes were dirty, probably from cleaning the house, Jordan thought. She had a huge red mark on her left cheek and she was cradling her left arm. She sat cross-legged on her bed, but didn't say a word. Didn't even look Jordan in the eye.

"What did they do to your arm?" Jordan asked gently.

He knew, even without knowing all the details. He had years of experience.

"Dad got mad that I wasn't working fast enough. He grabbed my arm and twisted it behind my back," she whispered quietly, her tears welling up with pain as the fire in her arm flared up, stubbornly refusing to dissipate.

"Let me see it," Jordan walked over to her bed and knelt beside it, "It looks like it's just twisted," he proclaimed after examining it closely, "It should be fine soon. At least it's not broken."

It was nothing he hadn't seen before. He had dressed enough wounds, fixed many a broken arm, he had become a pro, even better than a doctor.

They changed and got into bed, falling asleep more quickly than they would have thought possible. Jesse wasn't aware of drifting off, all she knew was that at some point during the night, she felt someone shaking her. She stared out in the darkness and sat up, using her right arm to prop herself up.

"What?" she asked sleepily into the darkness.

"Get up, we're leaving," Jordan whispered.

"What do you mean? Leaving? Where are we going?"

"I packed a bag for you. We are getting out of this house. We'll walk to South Dakota. We have some family friends there. They'll help us."

Jordan put a pack on her bed. He stared anxiously out the window. He was ready to get started.

Jesse stared at her brother for a moment, then reached for her clothes and began dressing as quickly and quietly as she could. One of the cool things about being a twin was that not a lot of talking was needed. Jordan knew that Jesse would never actually go against him, even though she sometimes liked to test him. Together, they sneaked downstairs and out into the night.

The two of them were shadows as they made their way up the mountain forest at the edge of the town. It was the place that every parent warned their children not to go.

"Hurry up, will you?" Jordan shouted to his twin sister, who was beginning to fall behind.

"I'm trying, but this stupid log tripped me!" she shouted back.

After she had caught up with him he said more gently, "Come on, we'll sleep over there tonight. We can make a fresh start in the morning," he pointed to a clearing straight ahead.

There were no trees and a little stream bubbled happily through the clearing. It was the perfect place to sleep. They would be safe there.

Along the way, Jordan picked up some sticks, ready to make a fire, his years at boys' camp finally paying off. When the fire was blazing and they were comfortably warm, Jesse brought out the snacks that Jordan had managed to scrounge up. They ate just enough to fill their stomachs for the night.

"Do you know where you're taking us or are you just wandering around hoping to find someplace?" Jesse asked as they were eating.

"Of course I know where we're going! We're going this way so we don't get caught and returned to our parents."

"Okay," she said, with a hint of suspicion in her voice.

She still wasn't quite sure if he really had a plan or if he had just snapped and was ready to get away from it all. She knew that he had been getting anxious to leave, knew that he would be leaving soon, it was only a matter of time. However, he wasn't much of a planner. He was a doer. Once he got something into his head, that was it, he'd do it, without planning what his next step would be. She would actually be surprised if he had any other plan after getting them this far.

Jordan cleaned up their mess as Jesse laid out the sleeping bags and the two of them fell asleep.

Chapter 3

Hunter, dressed all in black, so as not to be seen, scurried up the nearest tree and looked down at the picture he had below him.

Three men sat fishing by the river. Their things were scattered all over the place, making it look like a tornado had hit just that one spot in the forest. He scanned the sight carefully, looking for a bag that was in their possession. After locating it by a tree in the vicinity, he climbed stealthily down the tree and snatched it up- but not before one of the men saw him.

"Hey you! Bring that back!" a tall, strong, big boned man with a Texan accent yelled after him.

Hunter ran harder as the men got up and chased after him. He hid in a tree and waited for the pursuers to pass him. When the road was clear, he jumped down and ran in the other direction. Up ahead was a beat up, dilapidated, old woodshed. He approached it carefully, then curled up behind it and fell asleep.

Chapter 4

Saralee sat up groggily. Her once curly, brown hair, was now a tangled, dirty mess. Her clothes were full of dust and dirt and were ripped in several places. She looked like a street urchin in a movie she had seen as a child.

She was sliding across the room towards the dirty window when the door opened and a stealthy young man came in. As he walked towards her, she drew back with fear. Memories of what had happened last time someone had grabbed her were still fresh in her mind. She didn't want to find out if he was as mean as his partner had been.

"I brought you some food," he slid a plate of food across the floor towards her.

Saralee nodded her thanks. She kept a wary eye on her kidnapper as she reached for her plate. She began to eat, slowly at first, but as her stomach got used to the food, it demanded more and more. She was too involved in her eating to be too concerned with the fact that the man had come up to her. He knelt down beside her and examined her leg. As he touched it, she gave an unconscious jerk of pain, and began to back away from him.

"Ah, that doesn't look too good," the man said gently, easing his way back closer to her, "Let's fix this leg, shall we?"

Again, she nodded, unsure of how to answer. She hated that she wasn't able to speak. She had daydreamed about what she would do in such a situation, she always thought she'd be brave, be able to escape easily, at the very least be able to speak up, and yet here she was, a mute that cowered in the corner anytime someone came near her.

"What's wrong? Can't you talk?" the man asked.

She looked at him stupidly, then worked out some muscles in her throat as she found the voice that had been hiding from her since the first man had come in.

"Why are you doing this?" her voice sounded terribly weak, she cringed.

"The boss wants you healthy before we take you to her. Now, other than your leg, is there anything else that needs attention?"

Saralee shook her head again, uncertainly.

"Good. Now let's fix this leg."

He had brought in some wraps and some wood in order to splint her leg. She screamed in agony as he gently tried to set her leg. Fire was shooting up her leg and into her brain, making the world go black around the edges. He gave her some pain reliever to help ease the pain as he carefully wrapped her leg and attached the two pieces of wood to it. She was drifting in and out of consciousness as he worked, but she could still hear his tuneless humming. After he was done, he picked up the plated and his remaining equipment and left the room.

Chapter 5

Hunter opened the bag and gently took out each item. There were weapons, food, a laptop, a flashlight, extra clothes, a note, and a map. It was everything he needed to get. He would be able to go home now.

Quickly and gently, he put the stuff back into the pack and slung it over his shoulder. He was about to take off when he saw a face peering out at him through a cabin window.

Focusing his eyes, he saw that it was a young girl, about his own age. Her brown hair was pulled back in a ponytail, falling out around her face as strands of it tried to escape. She was wearing jogging clothes, and looked like she was in perfect health, if it weren't for her bright green eyes that were filled with pain, he would have believed nothing was wrong. He took an involuntary step towards her.

Saralee was standing by the window- looking out into the world she was now no longer a part of- when she saw him.

He looked like a normal teenage boy, with black hair and green eyes that looked so similar to hers. For some reason he stopped in his tracks and began staring right at her. Before she knew what was happening, he had walked up to the window.

"What's your name?" His voice revealed a slight accent that she couldn't quite place.

The sound traveled surprisingly well through the window and she noticed the gaps around the window panes, allowing sound to travel freely. Of course, it also allowed the wind to enter, which explained why she had been incurably cold since her confinement in the little room.

"Saralee," she said curiously, surprising herself with the fact that she could once again talk, "Who are you?"

"What are you doing here?" he didn't answer her question.

She thought for a moment, she didn't really have a choice if she wanted to be free, "I've been kidnapped," she said, she hoped that he would be able to help her. She was going to have to trust him. He was her only hope at the moment, "I don't know why or what they want. I don't know where I am or who they are either," she took a deep breath, trying to calm down.

Oh what she wouldn't give to be able to run right now.

"Anything else?" he asked, a hint of laughter in his voice.

She didn't know whether to be offended or relieved by his lack of anxiety or seeming sympathy to her plight.

"I've broken my leg," she said haughtily.

"Well, it seems you're in a bit of a pickle," Hunter nodded his head sagely.

"Thank you, Captain Obvious," man he was annoying, he got under her skin in the way only a sibling could, "Are you going to help me or not? Could you at least call the cops or something?"

She had wanted it to sound sassy and unbothered, as if she was just as unconcerned as he was, but it came out as more of a crying, childish plea for help.

"I'll see what I can do," he said with a shrug, not making any promises.

"Thank you."

She didn't know why, but she felt that being with him was a very good thing. His non promise made her feel safe, like she could breathe again. Like she was safe.

Chapter 6

"Wake up," Jesse yawned and awoke to Jordan's shaking. "What?" she asked as she sat up and blinked the sleep out of her eyes.

"We should move on."

She nodded and got to her feet. While Jordan went looking for something to eat, Jesse packed up camp. After she was done, she sat down to wait for her brother, hugging her bag close to her as she did so. It made her feel safe. She didn't like being alone. It was when you were alone that bad things happened.

While it wasn't too long, it seemed like an eternity to Jesse, before Jordan came walking back. His blonde hair was shining in the sun, looking more gold than blonde. Jesse let out a sigh of relief at the sight of the golden hair.

Both of their hair shone like gold in the sunlight, and their sky blue eyes held a heaviness that could only be known by those who had seen what they had seen, experienced what they had experienced. They had gotten their looks from their grandmother on their mom's side. Thinking about that made her mind drift to her parents.

The whole mess had started when they were twelve. She had Jordan never knew what had happened to change them, but one day it seemed like things were normal and the next, they started drinking, coming home drunk more and more until more often than not they lived in a drunken stupor. Then, the gambling started, and with it came their anger. The more they gambled, the more they lost, the more they lost, the angrier they got, and the angrier they got, the more they lashed out in a vicious cycle. Before Jordan and Jesse knew what was going on, their parents had changed into monsters.

They would neglect the twins for days on end, leaving them to fend for themselves. Those were the good days. Bad days they would find themselves treated like slaves, being forced to do whatever messed up chores came into their parents' twisted minds, or risk the consequences. Usually that meant a beating. It seemed like their parents had lived each day trying to come up with something new and horrible to do to their children. It was like a drug to them. They lived on in their childrens' pain, and the twins lived in a nightmare. That is, until last night, when Jordan had finally had enough.

"Ready?" Jordan asked, shaking Jesse out of her reverie.

"Ready," she confirmed.

A lot more than he thought had gone into that 'ready'.

Chapter 7

Saralee heard strange sounds, followed by the door opening and closing.

'One of them went to investigate,' she thought.

Moments later, she heard a struggle going on in the other room. The door opened and there stood the young man from the window. The one that, she realized, hadn't given her his name.

"Come on," he held out his hand, "We don't have much time."

She took his hand and off they ran. Or, more like hobbled. They hurried as quickly as they could to the stream where Hunter had gotten his supplies the night before. Once there, Saralee knew she had to stop. Her leg was in too much pain to go further.

"I can't," she panted, "I can't go farther."

"We can't stop here," Hunter glanced around, "They'll find us for sure."

"Then go on without me. If they come, I'll find a place to hide. I'm not your problem anymore, so thanks for the help. I greatly appreciate it. Good-bye."

Her confidence was coming back the longer she was away from them.

"Wait, wait, wait," Hunter shook his head, "Not happening," he emphasized the not, "I can't just leave you here to be found. You're my problem until I can get you safely home, or at least find someone else to do it. So, you're welcome for the break, but come on. We need to get moving. I'll carry you if I have to."

Without waiting for her to answer, he swooped her up onto his back and took off at a run. He didn't stop running till he reached a secluded pond. The area was surrounded by trees, so you could walk right past it and not even know that it was there.

"We'll rest here for tonight," he said breathlessly as he set her down gently.

"Thank you."

There was an uncomfortable silence as neither one of them knew what else to say to each other.

"Well, um, I'll go look for something to eat. Don't move."

"Where would I go?" she joked, looking down at her leg.

He unzipped his pack and gave her a knife, "For emergencies," he explained before leaving.

Taking advantage of his absence, Saralee used the pond to get cleaned up. Despite the fact that she was still wearing her dirty clothes, she felt refreshed and clean. Her hair was almost dry when Hunter came back with food and firewood.

As he was cooking she found the courage to ask, "Not to sound ungrateful, but why did you help me?"

He shrugged, "If you recall, you asked me for help. I couldn't very well say no, now could I?"

"Oh, so you did it for a clear conscience?" Saralee asked, trying to understand his motives.

"You could say that," he said with a shrug, as if it didn't matter to him why she thought he did what he did.

"I did," Saralee confirmed sassily, she felt as if there was something else going on, but she couldn't figure it out. She'd table it, and let herself reflect on it during tomorrow's jaunt, maybe the fast pace would work like running, "Now," she said, changing the subject, "You never told me, what's your name?"

"Hunter."

"How old are you?"

"Does it matter?"

"I'm 17," she said, trying to get him to open up by giving him details about herself.

"Good for you," he nodded.

"So, what brings you out to the middle of nowhere?"

"Just trying to help someone get something back that belongs to her."

"A girlfriend?" she pried, teasingly.

Getting him to talk was like trying to pull teeth. It was exhausting.

"She is a friend that is a girl, but no, not the kind of girlfriend that you're thinking of."

"Do you always do that?" she asked, her frustration coming to the surface.

"What?" he asked.

He honestly didn't seem to know what he was doing that bothered her so much.

"Say only enough to answer the question without any extra details?"

"Depends on the question."

"So, only personal ones?"

"Exactly."

"Why?"

He shrugged, "It's not anyone else's business. Here, eat this," he pushed a plate of fish and berries toward her.

As they ate, Hunter's mind wandered.

Chapter 8

Two Days Before

Hunter had been out for a ride when Felicia had come up to him, alerting him to the fact that her mother was looking for him and requesting his presence immediately.

He had quickly turned his horse toward the castle and raced to the study where Mara, the acting queen, was waiting for him.

"I need some help on something," Mara said.

He nodded. He figured this was what all this was about. He often got called in on assignments that other soldiers couldn't do. He had been born to spy, he was good at it. He often took assignments no one else could do, allowing Mara to run the kingdom in his stead.

"Flara's men have stolen a pack from me. I need you to get it back."

"What's so special about it?"

Pack retrieval wasn't usually in his area. Someone else could very easily go retrieve it.

"It has some special information. Information that could help us win this war that we're in. I have to get it back. It's vitally important."

Hunter nodded slowly, "Consider it done."

Mara breathed. WIth Hunter on the mission she knew everything was going to be alright. He was the best of the best. He had been training for this since he was a child.

Hunter hopped onto his horse and raced to his house.

"Cara!" he shouted as she rushed inside, grabbing his pre-packed bag. He was always ready to go, always ready for a mission, whenever and wherever it arose, needing very little prep time to get started.

"Hunter?" Cara asked, stepping out of the kitchen to see the blurred figure of the boy she had raised from toddlerhood, whiz past her.

"Mara's sending me to retrieve some information. I don't know how long I'll be gone," he explained, using as few words as he possibly could, as was his way.

Cara's heart plummeted to the bottom of her stomach. She tried to breathe through the discomfort, but it didn't work. After all these years, his profession didn't get any easier to deal with. Every time he went out on a mission, she once again wished that he had chosen a less dangerous profession. She hoped that one day he would actually decide to take up his crown and rule the kingdom, as was his right. She knew that Mara would stand aside the moment he said the word, but he didn't, and probably never would.

She knew he didn't feel like he could rule the kingdom, even though he had been born to rule. The loss of his family at such a young age had affected him. He needed answers, and he only trusted himself to find those answers. In a sense, it was a way for him to get some sense of closure.

"Be careful," she said softly.

"I always am," he gave her a quick hug goodbye and raced out the door, leaving the horse behind.

He had found horses to be more of a hassle than they were worth on these kinds of missions. He'd get back much faster on foot.

He had found Flara's men and the pack fairly quickly and easily. Probably one of the easiest missions he had ever been on. He was on his way back home when he had seen Saralee.

He couldn't quite place it, but there was something in her face, in her eyes, that reminded him of his sister. He didn't know why, but he had this feeling that he needed to keep her safe, to protect her. He had to rescue her.

Chapter 9

Close by, Jordan and Jesse were setting up camp for the night. Jordan was the first to see the smoke rising from the trees.

"What's that?" he asked, pointing to the smoke nearby.

"Probably just another camper's campfire," Jesse said with a shrug.

Jesse felt safer in the forest than she had at home, even though there were all kinds of horror stories about the forest that they were in now. She hadn't seen anything bad, any reason for such stories. She was beginning to think all those stories about the forest were just that, stories, meant to keep kids from going into the forest and getting lost.

"Let's check it out."

"Fine," Jesse shrugged, "Help me clean up."

They cleaned up quickly, eager to head over so they could meet their fellow campers.

Moments later, while sitting in the campsite, Hunter heard a twig snap, his mind coming back to the present. His body was trained for this, and needed very little thought from him. It automatically went into high alert, as only a person who spent most of his life in places he shouldn't be, doing dangerous things, can do.

Adrenaline pulsed through his body, conditioning him to

fight rather than to feel the need to flee. His past experiences had conditioned him well. In no time, he was on his feet, moving towards the noise. His hand at his waist, ready to draw the blade that was secured there.

"Who are you? What do you want?" Hunter demanded, a knife, trained warningly on each of the intruders.

The twins' hands flew into the air, their eyes became wide with both surprise and fear.

"N-n-nothing, I swear. We just came to say 'hi'," Jordan gulped and when Hunter didn't move to eviscerate them, he continued cautiously, "My name is Jordan. This is Jesse," Jordan jerked his thumb towards his sister, careful to keep his hands in the air, as not to cause alarm.

"We saw a fire and came over to meet you. We mean no harm," Jesse said.

"Hunter," Saralee said softly, "Put the knife down," she got to her feet gingerly and hobbled toward the newcomers.

Hunter slowly lowered his knives, ready to raise them again at any moment. Cautiously, the newcomers put down their hands.

"My name is Saralee," Saralee smiled at them, "The guy with the knife is Hunter," she held out her hand and each of the twins shook it in turn, "Have a seat," Saralee gestured them into their enclosure. As they sat down, she asked, "What brings you out here?"

"We are heading to South Dakota to see a family friend," Jesse said.

"So, you walk up a mountain and into a forest without any parental guidance?" Hunter asked skeptically.

He wasn't really sure about the world out there, that these three seemed to come from, but 17 seemed to be a young age to allow kids to just waltz through the forest without an adult. It was too young in his world, although an exception was usually made for him, for different reasons. Even in his world, most teenagers weren't like him. They didn't normally run to the woods when they were upset, or needed to think things through. They stayed closer to home.

"Truth be told," Jesse said, "We ran away."

She didn't feel like she was telling a big secret, after all, it seemed like Hunter already knew the answer. He knew that there was something going on, it was only a matter of time before he found out the truth. He just held that kind of vibe, a person that got what he wanted. And who knew, maybe they could help, at the very least it would be nice to have some other travel companions for a minute.

Jordan gave Jesse a warning kick. He didn't know that he was comfortable with his new companions knowing even that much about them and what they were doing in the forest. Maybe he was being paranoid, but he couldn't take that risk.

"What about you two?" Jordan asked, making sure his sister couldn't give out any more detail than she already had.

"I got brought here and am trying to find my way home," Saralee shuddered involuntarily as she remembered the small room, her terrible hunger pains, and those voices that had been planning something sinister for her. Something their 'boss' wanted done with her. Something she was supposed to be healthy for, which scared her even more than if they wanted her weak and broken, "Hunter ended up getting me out of the predicament I found myself in," Saralee continued, mentally shaking off the memories of the past several hours that had begun to snake around her, "I'm not quite sure on his story, but I think it has to deal with finding something for someone."

The three of them turned expectantly towards Hunter, waiting for him to fill in the blanks in his story.

"Like she said," Hunter said with a shrug, "I'm just trying to get something back for someone."

"What is this something?" Jordan asked.

"It doesn't involve you," Hunter replied shortly.

"Well, maybe we could help," Saralee replied.

"I doubt it," Hunter said, "I'm going to get firewood," he stood up and walked off.

"Why don't we join forces?" Saralee proposed while Hunter was gone, "We're all pretty much after the same thing. A way home."

Jordan and Jesse put their head together, using hushed tones in order to converse.

"We should do it," Jesse voiced.

"How do you know we can trust them?" Jordan asked.

"I don't know," she admitted, "But I trust them. They seem nice enough. And, after all, there's safety in numbers."

"Fine," he sighed, "But if anything goes wrong, anything at all, then we leave, okay?"

"Okay," she agreed. She could live with that, "We're in," she said to Saralee, before Jordan could take it back.

"Awesome," Saralee smiled.

"How did you break your leg?" Jordan asked after a moment of awkward silence.

Saralee looked down at her leg, "That predicament I told you about?" they nodded, "Well, the truth is, I was kidnapped, and the people who kidnapped me weren't very gentle," when all she got was slightly narrowed eyes, asking without words for more information, she added lamely, "I fell. When they pushed me, I ended up falling wrong and it snapped."

It was getting cold and the fire had died. Jordan and JEsse, who had planned their trip, were warmly dressed in jeans, t-shirts, sweatshirts, and jackets. Saralee only had the blue running pants and white tank top that she had been wearing on her jog. She crossed her arms firmly in front of her and held her entire body rigid. It was an instinctive action, one which gave some illusion of warmth. Noticing she was shivering, Jordan wordlessly held his jacket out to her. At that moment, Hunter came back with firewood.

"Staying the night," it was more of an acknowledgment than a question.

"Actually, they're going to join us," Saralee looked at him sideways, trying to gauge his reaction.

He shrugged, "As long as they keep up and don't get in my way," he bent down and expertly began striking flint against steel. In mere seconds he had a fire going.

"You're going to need some different clothes if you're going to survive traveling in the mountains," he said to Saralee.

He went to his pack and handed her some jeans, a t-shirt, a sweatshirt, and a jacket.

"Here, try these on. They'll be big, but they'll be better than what you have on right now."

She took the clothes and hobbled behind a bush to change. Her leg felt large and bulky. It made even the simplest motions seem insurmountable tasks. As she slid the pant leg up over her leg, she grimaced in pain. A rustling in the bushes made her jump and her heart leapt into her throat as a sense of dread built into her stomach. She was debating whether or not to scream when a bird hopped out of the bushes and cocked its head at her. Saralee took a deep breath as she yanked the pants up further and made her way back to the group.

"They're so huge on you," Jesse laughed, "You look so little."

"They'll be okay," Saralee smiled, brushing off her silliness at overreacting to the little bird. At least they were warm, "A belt would be nice, but it's fine."

"Here," Jesse said, reaching into her backpack, "My clothes will be a better fit, but you'll have to keep the sweatshirt and jacket," she handed some clothes to Saralee.

Saralee walked off, only to emerge from the bushes once more, looking much more like a proper human being this time. After confirming all was well with the clothes, and that they were all warm, they drifted off to sleep.

Chapter 10

"**G**one?! What do you mean she's gone?" shrieked Flara, her black robes billowing about her like a dark, wrathful ocean.

"It seems she has just...disappeared. We searched everywhere, but we couldn't find her," the deep boomy voice said.

"You idiots!" she stormed over to Boomy Voice, and then with a mock kindness said, "Rickstin, I gave you one little job to do," her voice rose until she was nearly yelling, "AND YOU LOST HER?!?!" then, her eyes fell on the young man that had fixed Saralee's leg, "And you," she growled, the young man shrinked back in fear, "I thought you said her leg was BROKEN!"

"It was...is..." he stammered uncertainly, he wasn't sure what was happening.

His heart was palpitating in his chest, and he could hardly breathe. Sweat began to pool onto his forehead, and he glanced around nervously, trying to find someway to escape, to shrink so tiny that they couldn't find him, to disappear.

Her voice became low with unconcealed menace, "Then how on Earth did she get away?"

"We assume she had some help escaping," the young man, whose name was Illian, stated with a gulp.

"Well, they can't have gotten far," Flara said, her voice returning to normal, "So, go find them and bring them to me."

She walked back to her chair and put her head in her hands for a moment as the men walked nervously, but gratefully out of the room. She was surrounded by idiots.

"Next," she said, taking a deep breath to get up some more strength to face the others.

Three dirty, smelly, beaten-up men came in and knelt before her.

"Rise and report," she sighed, already knowing that this wasn't going to go well.

Judging by the looks of things, they weren't coming with good news.

"A young man came in the night. He has stolen the pack," the biggest man said, coming forward.

"Hunter?" she asked.

Her blood boiled at the name. That filthy little mutt. He had everything in the world, and yet he threw it all away to be a spy, to run around the forests.

"We believe so, ma'am," the smallest confirmed, creeping forward, nervously.

"So. He is back," she whispered, speaking more to herself than to anyone else. To the three men in front of her she said, "Find him. And don't come back until you have him. Alive."

"He's quick," the medium-sized man complained, "There is no way we can get him here alive," he took a step forward to match the others.

He didn't want to do this anymore. They had already been bested once by the scrawny, little teenager, he didn't want to do it again.

"Break his legs. Knock him unconscious. Catch him in a bear trap- I don't care HOW you HARM him, just bring him to me," she said, listing off ideas, "I have reason to believe he is traveling with someone. A girl with a broken leg. Bring her to me alive as well. If anyone else tries to get in your way- kill them. Just make sure those two are alive," Flara returned to her seat and sat down imperiously, waving the group out.

Hunter had been in hiding recently, or so it had seemed, and now he was back, and most likely with her prisoner with the broken leg. She chuckled to herself. This was great news. He wouldn't slip through her fingers again.

"Blackheart!" she shouted.

"Yes, ma'am," the scruffy, muscular henchman came forward, bowing and staying on one knee.

"Rise. Come here."

She waited until he climbed the dais, closer to her than most were permitted, "I want you to assemble all of your men and search the forest. Hunter is back and possibly traveling with a brunette girl with a broken leg. I want them brought to me alive. You can do whatever you want to anyone who tries to get in your way."

"Right away, ma'am," he left the room, ready to assemble his men.

Flara smiled. She knew Blackheart wouldn't fail her. She was his best man, if she told him to do something, he got it done, no questions asked. He had been at her side from the very beginning. She trusted him with her life. He would get Hunter. By the end of the week she would have a way to destroy the rest of Hunter's precious world.

Chapter 11

J esse woke up to horrible images playing in her mind of her parents finding her and dragging her back to that house of pain and betrayal. She couldn't go back to bed, so she decided to get up and start packing up as much of the camp as she could. Hopefully they could leave as soon as the others woke up. She leaned up against a tree, staring out at the pond that was turning pink with the reflected light of the rising sun.

Hunter tossed and turned as he saw the images of his life flash before his eyes. He was standing there, watching as homes burned around him. One of them was his. His face was streaked with soot and his eyes burned as the smoke came towards him. There were people. Screams of pain. He looked around him. He was all alone. As the fire got closer and closer, Hunter woke up with a start.

He looked towards where the others had slept and upon seeing only two sleeping bodies, he quickly scanned the area and found Jesse. She was leaning against a tree, her feet dangling in the water. He walked up to her and sat down.

"Good morning, Hunter," she said cheerily as he plopped down beside her.

"Morning. Jesse, was it?"

"Yeah. What are you doing up so early?"

"I'm always up early on missions," he said succinctly, "You?"

"Nightmares kept me up. Decided to clean up camp so when you guys woke up we could head on out."

Hunter went to his pack and got out some paper and pen. They sat in silence, the only sound was the pen moving across the paper.

The sunrise made a beautiful picture. It painted the sky with pretty yellows, oranges, and reds. The light danced across the water, making Jesse's hair shine more golden than usual and lending a glow to her face. The dew evaporated as the sun's light touched it. It smelled like a beautiful spring morning, although it was early summer.

Suddenly, Hunter stood up saying, "We need to get a move on it."

He woke up Jordan and Saralee, got the camp packed up and they started off. They had to slow down so Saralee could keep up. For Hunter, the pace was painfully slow. So many people, unused to the pace he liked to keep and one of them wounded besides. They were slowing him down and he couldn't help wishing that they weren't with him.

He could have gotten to the portal so much faster were he on his own. Flara wasn't going to be taking her time. They shouldn't be either.

Chapter 12

The three men working for Flara had found the pond where the four travellers had spent the night. The grass was trampled from where the group had slept and the scent of campfire lingered in the air.

They searched the site, looking for any indication of who had been there and which way they had gone after they left camp. All they found was a pair of running pants.

"Ah, so she was here," a voice behind them said.

"Rickstin," the large one said, turning on his heels to face the oversized man with a formidable black beard.

"Brutus, Fobus, Mintus," he said, going from the biggest to the smallest.

They looked almost identical, except for their sizes. They all had scraggly dark brown beards and a receding hairlines. Their eyes were the color of burnt gravy and they smelled strongly of unwashed bodies and dirt.

"Let's go," Illian said, still hesitant about their mission, but not wanting to anger Flara any more than he already had.

He was the best looking of the lot. His dark brown hair was unruly and he had a stubby, unshaven chin, and crazy green eyes.

He also had a slighter build than the rest of them, making him look like the youngest on there, instead of the second oldest.

"Where?" Brutus asked.

"If she's with Hunter then they are headed to the portal," Rickstin said.

They would have to move fast. They needed to get there before the two kids did.

Chapter 13

Hunter let out an exasperated sigh as he stopped once more to wait for the other three to catch up. They had been walking for three hours and had only gone a couple of miles. At this pace, they would never make it to the portal before Flara and her men overtook them.

"Come on," he urged them, trying to keep the irritation out of his voice.

"We're trying, but Saralee can't go that fast," Jordan called back.

"We're moving too slow. We need to speed up," he said, once they had all caught up and they were together.

"We can't," Jordan said curtly, "Saralee is already going as fast as she can."

"Why don't you just leave me?" Saralee piped up, she hated being the one holding them all back. She should be faster. She was a runner, she had trained and trained, and yet she was going slower than anyone else, "I'll catch up sooner or later."

"We can't just leave you here," Jesse objected, scratching Saralee's back comfortingly, "We're a team now," she stopped her scratching and took Saralee's hand in solidarity.

"She's right. You're my responsibility until you're safe," Hunter said.

"Why are you in such a hurry anyway?" Jordan inquired.

"The people who kidnapped Saralee will be coming after us and at this speed we'll get caught. Now, how fast can you guys go with equipment?"

"We can go pretty quickly," Jordan said with some pride, "We made it here in three days."

"Good," he nodded, he began to hand packs to the twins, "You guys take these, "I'll carry Saralee."

Hunter swept Saralee up in his arms despite her protests and they were off. They were traveling much faster now, but he still wished the three of them weren't with him. He was used to working alone. It was comfortable. It was quieter. It was quicker.

There wasn't much of a trail and the tree branches kept hitting their faces, leaving little cuts. Fallen logs and big boulders tripped them up and slowed them down. It was uncomfortable for all parties involved, but they pressed on determindley.

Then, suddenly, Hunter stopped.

Chapter 14

"**B**lackheart, they're headed to the portal. Catch them before they pass through it," Flara barked into her walkie-talkie.

She laughed giddily. She was so close to her goal. She could taste victory and it was glorious. Soon Saralee and Hunter would be hers, and with them she would take the portal away from Mara. She would take back the power that was hers.

*

"They could be there already," Rickstin shouted at the group, getting anxious, "We need to hurry."

"What's the big deal?" Forbus yawned, "If they go to the portal, then we know where they are. We can go in and grab them, no problem."

He had just been recruited to Flara's army. He had no idea why they seemed so obsessed with getting the boy, or the girl, no idea about why the portal was so magical that they needed to beat the group to it.

"If they cross the portal they can get to Mara and they can form an army before we're ready to attack," Illian explained to Forbus.

He had seen the power of Flara. He had seen Hunter beat Flara over and over again, and her get more and more upset with each time.

"We'll be right behind them," Brutus said, also confused at the need and the rush to get to the portal.

"There is a magic there. Once they enter, it'll be closed to us. We won't be able to get in. They'll be able to create an army. We can't let that happen," Rickstin growled.

He was surrounded by idiots. He was always given the numbskulls, and expected to turn them into the best soldiers, and then tormented when they didn't get up to par. They were being idiots, asking stupid questions. They needed to pick up the pace. They needed to get to Hunter now.

Chapter 15

It was a gorgeous sight. Standing in front of them was a large waterfall, falling into a shimmering pool that looked like it was made of glass. On all sides there were rock walls that were covered in vines and flowers. They had walked through an arch in the wall behind them. Angled in the corner to their left there was a white bench swing, gently swaying in the breeze. On the right, hanging comfortably between the two biggest trees, was a hammock. Trees were scattered all throughout the meadow.

Hunter walked up and gently set Saralee on the hammock. Then he walked to the waterfall and started whispering and pushing at the wall.

"What's he doing?" Jordan asked Saralee.

"How should I know? Do I have the book on deciphering crazy behaviors from random boys you met in the woods yesterday?" Saralee grumbled, the pain in her leg making her irritable.

"You've known him longer," Jordan said, backing off and walking to his sister, "He's crazy," Jordan whispered into his sister's ear.

Jesse glanced at him, then back at Hunter. They watched him for a moment, trying to determine what it was that he was doing. After a minute, Jordan came to a decision.

"We should leave," he said softly, "I don't think I can trust someone knocking around on rocks like they're gonna talk to him."

Jesse hated to say it, but she knew he was probably right. However, she couldn't leave Saralee with this man. They were about to grab Saralee, when the wind changed, and the scent of wet grass was suddenly replaced with the odor of sweaty, unwashed bodies, and a side of bad breath. The travellers started to gag as five big, bulky men came into view.

Their faces were streaked with dirt and blood. Their hair was dirty and matted- not that Jordan, Jesse, Hunter, and Saralee looked any better, but at least they smelled better than the other group.

"You're right. You shouldn't trust him. What do you know about Hunter anyway?" Rickstin sneered.

"Oh, that's right," Forbus snickered, "You don't know a thing about him."

Hunter started to work even faster as he made a quick glance at the scene happening behind him.

"Why don't you come with us?" Illian said, holding out his hand invitingly.

Saralee's breath caught in her throat as she recognized her kidnappers. Slowly she began backing away from them, towards Hunter. While she may not know much about him, and he may be acting oddly, he still saved her once, she trusted him, and she found herself moving toward Hunter instinctively.

Hunter opened his pack and took out a knife, which he had put in his shoe. Then he pulled out two guns and another knife that he put in his belt. With one last great shove and a couple more words, the rock wall seemed to separate with a great creak. Impossibly, a perfect archway seemed to form where there had been solid rock a moment before. A strange mist shrouded the opening, obscuring anything on the other side of the archway from view.

The sound caused the five men in the clearing to lunge at the little group. Hunter threw his pack into the misty archway and ran towards his team as they made their way towards him.

Except for Saralee. In their haste to get away from the men, they had forgotten that Saralee wasn't able to run, that her leg was still broken. She was struggling to get to her feet from where she had fallen in her haste to try and get out of the hammock.

"Saralee!" Hunter shouted, as Mintus grabbed her from behind.

Hunter shot an arrow and got him in the arm, which made Mintus let go of her, giving Hunter the perfect aim.

Saralee collapsed and Jordan, who was watching the whole thing, picked her up and started to run toward the wall. Jesse took the lead, leaving Hunter behind to fight the other four men by himself.

Hunter shot Rickstin and Illian in the leg. Mintus received a shot in his side, causing him to crumble. Hunter took another knife out of his pocket and threw it, hitting another ruffian in the shoulder.

As he finished, he ran to the wall. As he moved toward it, the archway began to draw closer and closer together. Noticing, he began to run faster. As if it was taking energy from his movements, the opening shrunk still faster. Wildly, Hunter ran full tilt, giving it all he had. Even as he did this, though, he knew what the results would be. With a little thump, the archway vanished completely, leaving him alone in the meadow with the four injured men, and no way out.

Chapter 16

The trio turned around as the archway disappeared behind them. They were now alone in the strange place beyond the rock wall. They had no idea how to get back to familiar territory. They were lost. One by one, they turned back to take stock of where they were.

They were standing on a cobbled trail that stretched before them and around a bend that headed out of sight. The trees that lined the path seemed to whisper to them as the wind passed through the branches. The grass looked like a river of green as it blew about in the wind. It looked so soft and thick- just perfect to spend a lazy afternoon in. The whole place seemed to come alive in the wind.

"What should we do now?" Jordan asked.

"Well, we could follow the trail and find out where it leads," Saralee responded.

It was the only logical thing to do. They couldn't go back the way they had come, so that meant the only way to go was forward.

"It could lead us straight into a trap for all we know," Jordan snapped, his stress was getting the better of him.

He always had a hard time trusting the best in people, and letting go of that control. He always expected people to change, and not in a good way, just like his parents.

"Why would Hunter take us and himself into a trap?" Jesse asked, no matter what happened, she always wanted to believe there was good in people, she wanted to believe that people could change, and for the better, "He brought us here for a reason," she didn't truly know why, but she trusted Hunter, she knew he wouldn't bring them to a dangerous place, "So it must be somewhere we'll be safe."

"How do you know what Hunter would do? None of us even know who he is. Besides, he's not even here! This could all be some part of his master plan and he orchestrated it so those men would catch us there and that he would get locked out!" Jordan said passionately.

Suddenly, Jesse remembered something Hunter had done that very morning. HE had been writing something which he had put back in his pack after he had finished. If they could get it and read what it said, maybe they'd be able to figure out what to do. It was worth a shot at any rate.

"Hunter was writing some kind of note this morning..." Jesse started.

"So?" Jordan asked.

"Maybe he wrote down what we should do if we got separated," Jesse said.

"It's worth a shot," Saralee shrugged.

She had trusted him this far. She'd continue. She grabbed Hunter's pack and searched through the pockets. Inside the front pocket was a single piece of paper, torn from a notebook and folded into quarters. Looking around at her companions, she opened the paper and took a deep breath before beginning to read.

I don't think we'll be together for much longer.
It's only a matter of time before we are separated.
Hopefully things worked out like I planned
and you three are safely in the portal.
If not, try to find safety for the next 24 hours at which time
someone from the portal should be sent out to scout around.

When they arrive, tell them you were sent by me.
If you are in the portal follow the details listed below.

Your very lives are in danger, so it is essential that
you follow these instructions to the letter.
There is a map and some money in the same pouch as this note.
The map will lead you into town.
Once in town you need to find Cara's house.
Tell her that I sent you.
She'll help you with whatever you need.
Tell her that it is crucial for you to talk to Mara.
She'll be able to get you in.
You need to give this pack to Mara and ONLY Mara.
She'll know what to do with it.
One of them should let you stay with them.
If for any reason they can't or don't, take everything
you'll need to survive and head towards the forest.
In there you'll find a stream-
Stay as near to it as possible.
It'll be your only source of water.
Take care, be careful, and stay alive.
Hunter

"Okay, so I guess that's what we'll do," Saralee said after she had folded up the note.

Jordan opened his mouth as though to protest, but quickly closed it again upon realizing that he really didn't have a better idea.

They followed the trail until they reached the edge of town. There were many little shops set up in a circular fashion and people were walking about busily attending to their shopping needs. The air was humming with the sounds of people talking and birds chirping their tuneless songs. At the edge of all this there was a little opening, no bigger than an alleyway. They walked through it and saw houses scattered throughout the area in an almost grid-like pattern. Cobbled streets separated each side.

Trees loomed overhead, creating a canopy above their heads and providing enough shade to make it cool on a hot summer's day. At the end of the road, in the distance, stood the largest house any of them had ever seen. They withdrew the map from the pack and found the house they were looking for a ways down the street.

It was a little cottage with white walls and standing on a rock foundation. It was situated farther off than the rest of them. There was a wrap around porch with a swinging bench underneath a window, perfect for sitting outside to watch the sun go down. The entire house was trimmed with hunter green trimming and shutters. The door had a WELCOME sign hanging on it, decorated with two people sitting on a swing. The little group walked up the steps and knocked, the door swung open immediately.

A tall and slender woman opened the door. She had light brown hair, almost blonde and slightly graying. Her bright green eyes popped out in contrast with her very light skin.

"Can I help you?" Her voice had an almost childlike, musical quality to it. It made her seem younger and more vulnerable than she had appeared at first glance.

"Are you Cara?" Jesse asked.

"I am," the woman nodded. "May I ask you who you are?"

The village was a small one, one where everyone seemed to know everyone else, and it wasn't often that they got visitors.

"Jesse," Jesse said, holding out her hand, which Cara shook politely.

"Saralee," Saralee said, doing the same, with the same response.

"Jordan," Jordan said with a nod, keeping his hands planted firmly in his pockets instead of reaching out to shake hands.

"Well, it's very nice to meet you three. What can I do for you?"

"Hunter sent us," Saralee watched the woman closely, hoping to gauge what kind of reaction this woman would have to this name.

"Oh!" Surprise registered in her voice. "Well - come in." She stepped aside and waved them inside.

The room was fairly small. It had a river rock fireplace against the wall where a hearty fire was crackling. The fire brought out the deep blue of the couch and chairs that were sitting on top of a woven rug.

Above the fireplace was a picture of a young woman sitting in a brown leather chair, holding a young boy. To the left of them was a small coffee table and another woman sitting in an identical chair holding a baby in her arms. Standing behind them were two men, beaming proudly down at their little families.

"It's a nice place you have here," Jesse said politely as they sat on the couch.

"Thank you, Jesse," Cara said, sitting on the chair to the left. "But you said that Hunter sent you. Does that mean that something's wrong?" Worry had crept into her voice.

"Well, see... we're not exactly sure if something's wrong," Jesse answered.

"Where is he? Why did he send you here, but not come himself? I want to know everything that you know," she said, anxious to be filled in on the whereabouts of her adopted son.

"Well, we don't know where he is. He took us to this meadow and a... wall... opened... Then some men came and he told us to go through this... wall. So we did, but the wall ended up closing before he was able to get through. He left us a note that told us where to find you and that you'd be able to help us," Jesse explained sympathetically taking Cara's hand. "I'm sure he'll be here just as soon as he gets the wall opened again."

"No he won't," Cara said, shaking her head sadly. "He's gone." She let herself mourn for a moment, quietly wiping away a tear, before shaking off her somber mood. "So. What is it you need?"

"What do you mean, he's gone? Those men sounded like they were in a lot of pain. I'm sure he'll be able to get it open again without too much trouble," Jesse said.

"It's crucial that we see Mara. We have something we need to give her," Jordan stepped in, not wanting to waste any time.

"Well, you can't very well go see her looking like that," Cara said, rising to her feet. "Follow me." She floated down the hallway. She pointed to a door. "You guys can wash up in there." She walked on, taking them to another door and saying, "There are clothes in there- you can choose what you want. There should be something that fits right." She walked off, leaving them to their preparations.

It was a clothing wonderland. Never had they seen so many different clothes together in one place. So many styles, colors, and sizes. One could spend their entire life trying on clothes and never reach the end of them. Every kind of outfit imaginable was in that room, from shorts and t-shirts to evening gowns and tuxedos to flip-flops and high heels.

The wash room was just as amazing. There was a black porcelain sink with silver flowers engraved on it. The wall paper was dark and enchanting, with vines and flowers crawling up to the ceiling. There was a black clawfoot bathtub that was big enough to hold three people. It was mesmerizing.

The girls smiled, going through the clothes. It was like being a child all over again, playing dress up in the world's biggest closet.

Chapter 17

Hunter sized up his predicament. His back was to the wall and since the portal had closed, he had nowhere to run. That left him with nothing but rocks to defend himself with. There was no way he would be able to escape from the meadow without getting caught. The men were already getting up from where they had fallen when they had been hit.

Without thinking, he jumped into the air and clung to the lowest branch on the tree. Pushing himself backward and forwards, he swung his body until he was able to wrap his legs around the branch and cling to it with his hands and knees. Pulling himself upright on the tree branch, he started climbing up towards the sky. When he was high enough, he walked along the branch and jumped through the air to the other tree.

He leapt from branch to branch, tree to tree, until he reached the tree that was closest to the wall.

Unfortunately for him, the wall was too far down for him to land on and climb down to. If he decided to try such an undertaking, he'd probably end up breaking his leg. And that was if he was lucky.

He couldn't risk that. He needed his legs in good working condition. So, as nimbly as he had gone up the tree, he scampered down. His feet hit the ground running, all he had to do was make it to the entrance and he'd be free. They would never find him in the woods, and he could wait things out until he could get back into the portal.

Luck however, wasn't on his side. Illian managed to grab Hunter around the neck, pulling him downward. The rest of the group, minus Mintus, were on their feet, helping their comrade to bring Hunter down.

They tied him up and, using the rope to drag Hunter behind them, they left the meadow.

"Hold up you guys," Illian shouted to the rest of the group as they began to move faster and faster through the woods. "This little brat is difficult."

Hunter hadn't stopped fighting and dragging his feet for the entire time they had been walking, and it was beginning to tire Illian out.

The group stopped and made their way back to where Illian was struggling. Brutus rummaged through his pack, finding something to knock Hunter out. Hunter tried to back away from it, but the men were too strong for that. They forced the powder into Hunter's face.

He struggled to stay awake, struggled to keep the edges of unconsciousness from taking hold of him completely, but it was a useless task. The darkness took over him and they carried him to Flara's citadel.

Hunter woke up just in time for them to reach the front of her huge, stone mansion. There were black flags flying from every place that could conceivably hold a flag. There was an air of darkness and unhappiness in the atmosphere surrounding the place. The cold stone construction just added to the gloominess.

There was no sun. It hardly ever reached that far into the forest, and that lack of light created obscene shadows that made the citadel seem even more formidable and evil than it would if it had been placed somewhere else, with more sunlight. What little light was there, was quickly dampened by the trees that were looming overhead, making it nearly impossible to see anything.

The outside of the mansion was cluttered with people sharpening knives, axes, and swords. The screeching sound of the sharpening took over everything. It was overwhelming. It caused Hunter's ears to ring in pain. They reached the doors, which opened automatically as they walked up.

Forbus shoved Hunter into the lobby. It was a tiled room that held nothing but soldiers. It was cold and Hunter's hatred of being in Flara's lair grew within the pit of his stomach and threatened to burst. He was shoved up the stairs to his left and then he was pushed into a dark room at the top of the stairs.

The full-length windows were covered with dark drapes. The only light in the room came from a chandelier that hung above them. Soldiers lined the walls. There was a stage like area in the front of the room where Flara sat, like the drama queen that she was. There was a ring right in front of the stage. It was known as the circle of death in the mansion. It was where the prisoners were forced to stand as their punishment was given out. Hunter was pushed into that circle.

"Hunter, so we meet again," Flara said, her eyes sparking in delight.

He gave her a murderous stare, but didn't say anything.

"You knew it was only a matter of time before I got a hold of you. After all, one can only run for so long."

"You're right," Hunter conceded. "But unless your security has gotten 300 times better-" he glanced around the room at the soldiers. Security looked a little tighter than before, but not by much. "You won't have me for long," he spat out his assessment of her security.

"That ego of yours will get you into trouble some day."

"If my ego will get me trouble," Hunter asked curiously, "What will your hunger for power get you?"

"It will get me your precious little world," she said simply as she strode up to him and began to walk circles around him. "I will see it crumble around you." She leaned close to his ear and whispered, "Again."

"You'll never get in!"

"We'll see. After all, you are going to help me," she sneered. "My pet," she stroked his cheek and he turned away in disgust.

"I will never help you. You're a killer and I will see you rot before I help you!" Hunter seethed.

"Guards! I think he needs a little time in the prison to help him see things my way."

The guards put handcuffs on him and dragged him out of the room, down the stairs and into the prison. It was cold and damp. It smelled so strongly of mildew that it made Hunter gag. They threw him into a cell and left him there.

Chapter 18

It was amazing what a shower could accomplish. Saralee felt more refreshed than she had in days. Dressed in a dark blue tunic with a black leather belt around the waist, and black Capris, she felt ready to take on the world. She walked into the front room and saw Jordan sitting on the edge of his seat on the couch by the fire. He glanced up when she walked in.

"I don't know about this," his voice laced with worry that he was trying to hide, "We don't know what we're getting ourselves into. I mean, we don't even know who this Hunter person is, but we're just going to go ahead and do whatever he tells us to?"

"I get it," Saralee nodded, "You don't trust people, especially people you just met. It's normal, but sometimes you just have to have some faith. You have to trust people. Hunter saved my life. He wouldn't do that if he was the evil person that you think he is. He would never purposely send us somewhere dangerous. Following his orders is the least we can do. I think, that after all he's done, we can at least trust him," she sat down on the couch next to him.

"Hey guys," Jesse said, coming into the room.

She walked in, and twirled around to show off her new outfit. It had been ages since she had a new outfit, and she felt like a queen in her black jeans and red shirt with flowy sleeves that she couldn't help playing with.

"You look very nice," Saralee said, standing up and hobbling over to her.

"Yes, you all do," Cara said, walking into the room, and giving each of them a once over "Now we should probably go find Mara."

Cara led them into the town. It was the kind of town one would find in storybooks. Little cottages lined cobbled streets. The smell of freshly baked bread wafted toward their noses. People were talking and exchanging goods. Jordan slowed as they passed the bakery, looking longingly at the bread as his stomach let out a dying whale sound, Jesse smiled understandingly at him, and gently dragged him along. They didn't want to lose Cara, and she was a woman on a mission.

Cara didn't stop until they had reached the edge of town. The house they finally stopped at was a mixture of an overly large cottage and a small mansion. It was the largest building they had seen in the entire town. It was the house for someone of influence, while still keeping with the integrity of the rest of the village.

The trio of teenagers stood back, looking at it in awe, while Cara knocked sharply at the door. A guard was swift to answer the call.

"Cara," the soldier asked in surprise, shaking it off quickly.

There was a time that Cara was at the castle all the time. At the beginning, while they were all still struggling after the incident, Cara had practically lived there. However, that was a long time ago. Mara and Cara had agreed to allow Hunter to live a more normal life. A life where he wasn't reminded of his family's tragic story everywhere he went. Cara had moved Hunter out, back to her own little cottage, and tried to stay away from the castle as much as possible.

"How can I help you?" he asked.

"I need to see Mara," she said coolly, as if this was simply another day and nothing out of the ordinary was happening.

After taking a moment to process what was going on, he stepped aside and allowed Cara and the trio of teenagers to pass. Cara lead them through the vestibule and down a long hallway and into the farthest room to the left.

The room was big enough to hold Cara's entire cottage in. Floor to ceiling windows let all the light in without need of any electricity. The sunlight seeping into the windows caused rainbows to dance across the floor, making the floor look like it was a gentle moving river, that sparkled in the light. There was a raised platform where a chair sat. It was expertly engraved, fit for a queen. On the chair, sat the most beautiful person any of them had ever seen.

Part of her goldish brown hair was caught up in a bun like fashion, while the rest of it encased her shoulders. She had a natural blush on her cheeks, giving it a pink touch that off set her stormy blue eyes. With her shimmering blue dress, she looked almost magical sitting there.

"Cara," she said. Her voice had a musical, lilting quality to it, "It's nice to see you."

She flowed up towards them. As she approached them, her arms opened to allow Cara to step into them.

"Hello Mara," Cara replied as they pulled out of the embrace.

"Hello Cara. What news of Hunter?"

"That's why I'm here, actually."

Mara nodded, she knew Cara well enough to know that this sudden and unexpected arrival could only mean there had been some news of Hunter that hadn't yet reached Mara's ears.

"What's happened?" Mara's heart dropped to her stomach.

She hadn't thought that this mission was that dangerous. Hunter should have been able to find it, and get back fairly easily. Had she overestimated him? Underestimated the danger? What had she done?

"These children say they have news of him," Cara stepped aside and let full view of the teenagers.

Mara eyed the trio, finally seeing them. Something looked familiar about Saralee. With her attention already drawn to Saralee, she chose to speak to her, "And what news is that?"

Mara remained calm. She couldn't freak out right now. She knew she needed to get facts before she could come up with a plan.

She had to think through logically. She was their ruler after all, and she couldn't go off half cocked.

"Well, um," Saralee responded, she curtsied almost flawlessly.

Her parents had drilled proper etiquette, along with sports, into her head from a young age. She could curtsy with the best of them, and then beat them in a game of basketball.

"Please, don't do that," Mara waved off the gesture. Being the youngest she had only been bowed to if someone higher ranking than her wasn't in the room, which wasn't often. Even after all the years of being the acting reigning ruler, she couldn't get comfortable with people bowing to her, so she had long ago gotten rid of the practice, only using the practice with outsiders, "What news do you have of Hunter?" Mara pressed, allowing Saralee to continue.

"Well, at the meadow he told us to go through the portal, but there were these guys that came after us. He fought them off to give us time to get in, but the portal closed before he was able to go through it. He wrote us a note telling us to give this pack only to you," Saralee said, handing Mara the pack.

"Thank you," Mara's voice was sad.

"I'm sure he'll be here soon, just as soon as he is able to open the portal," Jesse said, trying to comfort her, just like she had with Cara, "The men were pretty hurt, so he should be able to open it without much trouble. He should be here soon."

"That's not going to happen," Mara's voice held a sense of worry, "He won't be coming. He's on his own."

"Both of you said that," Jordan said, looking curiously between both Cara and Mara, "Why?"

"Once the portal closes, there is no way to open it again for a day and half. He can't get back, at least not for another 24 hours," Cara explained, "We know those men. We know their leader. The chances of him being able to escape are slim," unshed tears made her eyes bright.

Sadness invaded the room as the realization of what happened, dawned on them. Hunter had sacrificed himself for them.

Chapter 19

Hunter paced his cell. He had a rhythm going. Two steps, turn, four steps turn, two steps, turn, four steps, and on and on and on. It made for a rhythmic tone that was nearly hypnotizing if you listened to it long enough. However, even the calming rhythm he had going wasn't enough to keep the sense of dread from creeping over him and settling into his stomach.

He needed wide open space, he hated spending too much time indoors, and a 2 by 4 cell was driving him mad. That sense of being vulnerable was overwhelming. He hadn't felt like that since he had watched his father die, and his mom get taken away by Mintus. Even though he had been a mere child, that night he had vowed that he would never let himself feel that way again.

Getting tired of his pacing, and the too steady rhythm he had created, Hunter fell onto the mattress that was in the far corner. The straw poked him uncomfortably in his back, but he didn't care. He was too busy trying to plan his escape. His first step was to get his handcuffs off.

An idea popped into his head, he got to his feet and shouted out, "Hey, you! Come over here!"

A young man with straggly, dirty blonde hair and mustard stains on his shirt came up to him, a hot dog in his hand.

"What do you want?" he asked with a southern accent.

"Can you take these handcuffs off?"

"No," the man said simply, taking a bite of his hot dog, mustard spilled onto his shirt as he did so.

"Why?" Hunter shrugged, "It's not like I'm able to go anywhere. I'm in a cell. The handcuffs are just overkill."

"Boss' orders."

"What? Does she think that by taking my handcuffs off I'll suddenly have magic and be able to disappear into thin air?" he laughed at the ridiculousness of that thought.

The young soldier gave it some thought, then walked back to get the keys and walked back to Hunter.

"Give me your hands," he barked.

"You won't be able to get them off like that- you need to take them off in here."

"Fine," he sighed. He unlocked the cell and stepped inside.

As soon as the handcuffs were off, Hunter grabbed the keys from the man's hands. Hunter pushed the soldier onto the mattress and ran out of the cell, locking it behind him so that the young man couldn't follow him.

It was time to once again make a break for it. It was easier than last time. Almost too easy. That was making Hunter nervous.

Chapter 20

"That's it? You're just going to leave him there?" Saralee asked, disbelief in her voice.

"There's nothing we can do," Mara replied, she kept her voice steady.

With Hunter, she had lost another member of her family, and that was like a knife to her heart. She had lost so much in that fire. Flara had caused so much damage, so much pain. Hunter was now another person to add to the list of people Flara had taken from her.

"You have to do something," Saralee said, "We can't just leave him there to die!" she was shouting now, with tears coursing down her face.

She was feeling a sense of loss and panic that she couldn't quite explain. She normally wasn't one for such high emotions, but it was like this news suddenly brought up all the emotions she hadn't felt before to the surface to make her face them now. It was an emotion she knew that not even running for miles would get rid of.

"Hunter saved her from two of those men," Jesse explained to Cara and Mara, who were looking at her strangely, as she went over to comfort Saralee.

Mara nodded, and rang a bell by the door. A young woman came in. His shoulder brown hair was nearly identical to that of Mara's.

Her simple blue tunic made her look battle ready at a moments notice. Her soldier like quality was offset by her sympathetic blue eyes. Those eyes drew you in, made you trust her, and want to tell her all of your secrets and problems.

"Felicia," Mara smiled lovingly at the girl, "Will you take this young lady up to one of the guest's rooms and give her something to calm her down."

The girl nodded and was about to take Saralee out of the room when Mara added to her request.

"While you're at it, why don't you get the doctor to see what he can do for her leg?"

"Alright," Felicia took Saralee by the arm and led her out of the room.

Felicia gently led Saralee to the doctor while she went to find some tea to help Saralee relax. Felicia's heart was heavy. She had heard every word that had been said. She had seen Cara come up to the castle with the three teenagers, and had slipped into her hiding spot in the throne room mere moments before they had. Maybe she'd make some tea for herself as well. She could use something to help her push through and finish her work.

Chapter 21

Hunter slipped quietly out of the prison and up the stairs, running to the door and towards his freedom.

Getting through the corridors was easy, hardly any soldiers roamed the hallways. However, once outside, things got a little tougher. People were all over, milling about, half armed, half relaxed. He would have to take great care.

Moving as quickly and quietly as he possibly could, he crept along the edge of the fort, ducking in and out of bushes and trees as people meandered around outside. He had plenty of practice becoming invisible, nothing more than a shadow, and that technique aided his quest.

He had just crossed outside of Flara's lair when someone grabbed him from behind. He fought as hard as he could but his captor was stronger with every bit of struggle the grasp got tighter and tighter, until his ribs began to hurt from the pressure being put upon them. He was dragged back to the fortress, to Flara.

"I caught him trying to escape," his captor said in a deep voice.

"Thank you, you may leave," Flara waved the soldier away, "Looks like someone has been a naughty boy," she teased, "Tsk, tsk, tsk. Too bad your little plan didn't work, because now you'll have to pay for that, and for all the other times you've slipped through my fingers."

Hunter said nothing. He kicked himself for letting himself believe that he was free- it had been too easy. He should have known it was some kind of trick, a trap. He had allowed himself to get cocky, to underestimate her. That was dangerous.

"Ah, the little snake has nothing to say," her voice was sickening to his ears, "Guards!" she cried, "Take him to the chamber and prepare him," she said maliciously.

A guard pulled his arms painfully behind his back and once again put him in handcuffs. The soldiers took great delight in jerking Hunter to his feet and dragging him down to the chamber. They went down, past the prison where he had just escaped, down, further and further until Hunter was sure they couldn't go down any further, and yet they did.

As long as it had taken to get there, Hunter wished that they had never gotten there when he finally got to see the chamber.

Chapter 22

"Follow me," Mara said as she led them twins across the hall into a more comfortable looking room.

While it was still large, it had more of a homey feeling to it. It was less, 'let's get down to business' and more 'let's discuss ideas' feel to it. There was a fire going in the cobbled fireplace, illuminating the bookcases that lined the room.

Mara gestured toward the oak table and the leather seats surrounding it, "Have a seat."

The twins did what they were told and quickly found seats next to each other.

"What has gotten you involved in all of this?" Mara continued once they were all seated.

"Well, we were going to find family when we met up with Saralee and Hunter. It was Saralee's idea that we should join forces," Jesse explained.

Jordan sat in silence, but let her continue talking.

"Ah," Mara nodded in understanding.

Mara started rummaging through the pack she had placed on the table. She examined the contents of the bag carefully.

"So, what's up with Hunter?" Jordan asked as Mara read the note, "Who is he? Why is he so important?"

"Jordan, shush," Jesse whispered.

Mara and Cara seemed to be very close to this Hunter person, and they had just been told that he might not be coming back. Now was hardly the time or place to be hounding them with questions about him.

"No, I think we have the right to know what's going on here. After all, this affects us too," Jordan wouldn't let Jesse keep him quiet.

He didn't care. He wanted answers. Right now he was feeling like he was back with his parents, purposely being kept in the dark as a way of control. He hated it. He had gotten them out of the situation, and he wasn't going to let himself be dragged back into another one.

"I agree," Mara stated, shocking both Jesse and Jordan, "You do have a right to know, however, now is not the time nor place for it," Mara stated, "In time, you will be told, but for now, all you need to know is that Hunter is our best man and a very good friend of ours," Mara set down the note on the table and picked up the map.

"Can we do anything to help?" Jesse asked, as she tried to stifle a yawn.

"It's late, and you've had a long and very eventful day," Cara said, noticing their red, puffy eyes and their stifled yawns, "Why don't you just get some rest and we'll talk in the morning?"

Once more, Mara rang a bell, and Felicia came in and took them to their rooms. All could be brought to light in the morning.

Chapter 23

Hunter laid on his side in the dark and damp room. The coldness seeped into his bones. Above him, a lone light flickered on a chain. It was barely bright enough to keep him from being completely overcome by darkness; hardly light enough to allow him so see the hand in front of his face, let alone anything else in the room.

Turning onto back so that he could use his hands, he pushed himself up off the floor. Once on his feet, he made his way to the walls, and found a door. Adjusting his body so that he could reach the handle and still see what he was doing, he tried to open it. It wouldn't budge. He moved onward, finding another door. This one he found success. With great difficulty, he managed to force this one open. The creak was earsplitting.

He walked in cautiously. More lights illuminated this room, but it wasn't a comforting light. It was just a light that showed off the horrors that would await him in that room. A deep sense of knowing filled his bones. Flara would put him in this room; would torture him in this room. Although he would rather not, he had to know. He looked around. He had to know what he was going to have to deal with.

Whips and rods hung on the walls like trophies while chains

hung from the ceiling like streamers. The heat from the fireplace made the whole room seem like it was shimmering. He had only been in there for a few minutes, and already he was drenched in sweat. He was just about to go back the way he had come, when he saw a door on the other side. Drawn to what could possibly be behind it, Hunter took a step toward it.

He tried to push it open, but it was locked. He struggled, but it refused to budge. Nothing left to do. Nothing left to see, Hunter made his way back to the chamber.

He was about to continue with his investigation when the door he had tried to open first, opened and Flara, dressed in her usual black, came in. Her long hair was tied back. She was dressed to torture someone. Her eyes danced with delight as the excitement of what she was going to do slipped out of her eyes.

"Doing some exploring are we?" she asked, stepping into the room.

The door banged shut behind her, making sure that there way Hunter would be able to escape the way she had come.

"What do you want Flara?" he hissed as she walked closer.

"You know what I want," she smiled sweetly, almost innocently, as he stepped into the circle that lined the floor.

"I don't have it. Mara does, and even if I did, why would I give it to you?"

"You still think this is about the pack?" she laughed, "You aren't as smart as I thought you were. The pack is old hat. This is about you and your family now."

"You'll never lay a hand on them. They're protected in a place you'll never see again in your sad, pathetic life."

"Ah, you've forgotten," she said almost sadly, "It's understandable. You were only a little thing then."

"I will never forget that day! You destroyed a town," he seethed.

That terrible night was forever branded in his memory. He could still feel the heat of the fire. He could still hear the screams of people as their lives were torn apart. His dreams were filled with his father dying in front of him. The look of his mother's face as she saw his dead body, and while she was dragged away was forever branded in his memory. He couldn't see Mintus' face without remembering that night. It was the night that his father, uncle, and adopted uncle were killed. It was the night he lost his sister and his mother. No, he would never forget that day. It was forever branded in his mind.

"Then you'll know, I'm only missing one piece of the puzzle."

"You don't know where she is," Hunter said confidently.

His sister had been taken away. A couple had taken her out of his world. They had raised her in a world that had nothing to do with Flara or the portal. The couple would take care of her, they would keep her safe.

"She's safe from the likes of you," Hunter set his jaw.

"Ah, but that's where you're wrong. I have already located her. All I need to do is pick her up."

Hunter sat in stunned silence. They had found her? She'd be about 17 now he thought. His mind whirled, going to the most logical place. No, he shook his head. It couldn't be. It was just a trap. He had spent years searching for her. Mara and Cara had refused to tell him where she was, he wasn't even sure if they knew for sure where she was at. There was no way Flara had been the one to find her. Leana and Pete were too smart for that. It had to be a lie. She was just toying with him, trying to get him to tell her something, to bargain with her in order to keep his sister safe.

"I thought so," Flara jeered.

"You don't know anything about her," he said vehemently, "It's a lie."

"Tsk, tsk, tsk. Not trusting me is a big mistake, so is underestimating me."

"Trusting you would be an even bigger one."

"You have no idea who you're dealing with."

"I think I have a pretty good idea. If you recall, I was there that night. I've gotten through your fingers on multiple occasions."

Flara started to prickle, she hated being reminded of her loses, especially by this little brat. She slapped him across the face and stormed out of the room. She'd let him stew on the information she had just given him. Once it was nice and pounded in his head, she would go to work.

"You three take him back to prison. Take off his handcuffs, but make sure there are three people guarding him as you do so. DON'T let him escape again," she told the guards that were outside the door before she stormed off.

Chapter 24

Saralee woke up to light streaming into her room. The bed was so soft. All she wanted to do was curl up underneath the light blue fleur-de-li patterned quilt that was covering her, and go back to sleep. Keeping her eyes partially closed, she examined the rest of her room.

Lacy blue curtains were blowing in the breeze, bringing with it fresh air. Saralee took a deep breath, her eyes falling on her nightstand where a white lamp illuminated some pulls and a glass of water. She took them gratefully and walked toward the window. There was a stream outside her window that caught her attention.

It gurgled happily as it skipped over the rocks on its way to some unknown location. The trees seemed to hover over it, like a bodyguard trying to keep it away from all the dangers of the world beyond. As she looked at it, she couldn't help but be reminded of all that Hunter had done for her.

She was jerked from her reverie by the door opening and someone coming in. Saralee remembered her as the girl who had taken care of her last night. She was once again in a simple tunic and had her hair pulled up into a braid. Even in the simple garb, she looked only slightly less dazzling than Mara.

"Hi," Felicia said, putting a tray of food on the desk, "How are you feeling?"

"Better thanks," Saralee smiled, "It's Felicia, right?"

"Yeah," Felicia nodded, her braid slipping over her shoulder, "Does your leg feel any better?"

"A lot better," she said, amazed, "And it's a lot easier to walk around now too."

It still felt bulky and strange, but not nearly as much as it had the past several days. The doctors here really could work miracles.

"The doctor made you a proper cast for your leg, which will let you be able to move faster and better than with that crude splint you had on when you got here," Felicia explained away the magic.

"Thanks," Saralee said, "I'm sorry that I acted like a total fool yesterday. It's just that Hunter...well, he, he rescued me, and he did all he could to keep me safe. Now, all of a sudden, he's gone and no one seemed to be doing anything, and it was like no one cared, and I just..." she didn't know how to finish her sentence, so instead she picked at her food.

"It's perfectly alright," Felicia validated, "We understand. Hunter is dear to us all. Him not making it back is hard for us all to handle. But he's strong, and this is hardly our first rodeo," Felicia explained, "Now eat your breakfast. I'll come back for you later," she walked out of the room.

Saralee picked at her fruit and bread, not really tasting or caring about the food. She was too deep in her own thoughts when Jesse came into her room with a hop in her step.

"Hey you. How are you doing?" she asked, kneeling beside Saralee's chair.

"I'm much better. What makes you so cheery?"

"Good. That's good," Jesse nodded, "Today is a beautiful day. You can't be upset on a day like this."

The sun was shining, she was free, life was good. Any little reason was enough to celebrate. She had learned that a long time ago. Find something good, and celebrate it.

"Hunter is gone. We're in some strange place. We don't know anyone here, and if that wasn't enough, there is no way to leave. How is it, through all of this, you can still be such a happy person?"

All she wanted was to go home. Her parents must be worried sick about her. She felt just as imprisoned now as she had back in the cabin. It may be a different jail cell, but it was a jail all the same.

Jesse thought a moment about Saralee's question. What made her like that? When her world had first gone south, she had been bitter and moody and even her brother couldn't cheer her up. Nobody wanted to be with her. She was a giant cloud of anger and bitterness.

However, gradually, she began to realize that being bitter and mad about things she couldn't change wasn't going to do anything but hurt herself. It wouldn't change their situation. So, while her brother gained trust issues and over-protectiveness, she gained trust in others, a cheerful disposition and a need to help others out when they were hurting or had a problem. She didn't want anyone to feel like she had, so she didn't herself.

She wasn't able to answer the question before Felicia came in with Jordan.

"Well, let's go," Felicia said.

"Who are you?" Jordan asked as they all walked down the hallway.

He knew her name was Felicia, but he didn't know how she fit into the picture. He didn't really know how anyone fit in, and that bothered him. Mara was like queen, he had guessed, and Hunter must be a soldier, a very high ranking soldier apparently, but he had no idea how Cara and Felicia fit in. They had to fit in somehow, but as far as he could tell they were just extra pieces in a puzzle.

"Name's Felicia," she shrugged, opening the door to the library she added, "I'm Mara's daughter."

The trio froze, staring at her blankly. Mara's daughter? Daughter? She didn't act like she was going to be a queen, wasn't treated like a princess. But, they couldn't deny that she certainly did look like

Mara. After being told, it wasn't hard to see the resemblance. Shaking off their confusion, they stepped into the library.

Books. Books were everywhere. The walls were lined with bookcases, looking like soldiers standing at attention. Every window had a window seat all set up, perfect for curling up in and getting lost in a story. Cara and Mara were already there, waiting for them to discuss plans.

"I see that you've all gotten to know my daughter, Felicia," she said, seeing their still shocked faces.

"Yes, we have," Jesse assured her, as Jordan and Saralee simply nodded their heads.

"Good, since that is out of the way, let's get down to business," she pulled out the map and put it on the table. They leaned in to get a good look at it, "Flara's fortress is somewhere around here," Mara said, drawing a circle with her finger, "But she has forts and soldiers all throughout here," this time the circle was longer.

"So, what do we do?" Saralee asked.

Jordan looked at his sister and the stranger they had picked up. While Jesse seemed more reserved about the plans, Saralee looked ready to jump into whatever was going on with both feet. Jordan however eyed Cara and Mara trying to figure out what their endgame was.

"We need your help. We are getting ready for war. We've been dealing with skirmishes with her for years, but the pot is now boiling over, and it's going to explode. We need to be ready for it when it happens."

"What?" Jesse gasped, before she pursed her lips shut and seemed to shrink back into herself.

"How can we help? We don't know anything about fighting," Saralee jumped in.

"You'll be trained," Mara explained gently.

"Why?" Jordan asked.

"What do you mean, why?" Mara asked.

"Why do you need us?" Jordan reiterated, then continuing with

71

his questioning he asked, "How do you know you can trust us? How do we know we can trust you? You could be the bad guys."

"You guys are special. We need you. Once you start, you'll realize why you are needed here to help us," Mara said.

"And as for you trusting us, we're all you've got. Hunter trusts us, so if you trust him, then you can trust us too. As for being able to trust you, well, Hunter kept you with him and he sent you to us for a reason. He wouldn't do that kind of thing if he had any doubts about you, your loyalties, or intentions. That is a rare thing for him, so if he trusted you, we do too," Felicia replied.

The three of them glanced at each other in surprise. That was more than she had said since they had met her. She had Hunter's way of answering a question with as few words as possible.

"So the question is, will you help us?" Cara asked.

"Doesn't look like we have a choice," mumbled Jordan, wondering if he had gotten into a worse position than being with their parents.

"Yes, you do have a choice. We won't force you. It's up to you, but know this, we do need your help," Mara said.

"I'm in," Saralee said enthusiastically, practically jumping out of her seat as she said that.

At least it would be getting her out and doing something. She'd be able to do something physical, be a part of a team again, to feel like her old self again. Of course she was in.

"Me too," Jesse said quietly.

"Alright, I'll help," Jordan responded after thinking it over.

He just prayed that he hadn't just led his sister into destruction.

"Thank you," Cara said, standing up.

"Felicia, dear, take them out to the stable and the rink and let's start their training," Mara said.

Felicia quietly did as she was told.

Chapter 25

Although Hunter was back in prison, he felt victorious. He had hit a chink in Flara's armor. He could do this. He could bring her down. Hopefully with minimal bloodshed.

He laid himself down onto his uncomfortable mattress. He didn't care that the straw was sticking him in the back. He was too busy working on how to get rid of Flara, and regain his freedom.

The sound of something scurrying about caused him to jerk his head over to the left. He scanned the wall. A yellowing piece of paper attached to some bark was being slid into his cell from a small hole. Hunter had overlooked it in his previous scan of his surroundings, as it was small and blocked off by a corner of the mattress. One would have to know what they were looking for in order to find it.

He picked up the piece of paper. Careful not to rip it, he unfolded it.

That was a stupid thing to do.

What? Hunter scribbled back, and pushed it through the hole.

Trying to escape.

No, it was foolish of me to underestimate Flara.

She'll have you tortured to no end for this insult.

It's nothing new.

Be more careful.

Who are you to tell me what to do?
No one, just a person who has been here for a long time.
I can handle myself. I'll be fine.

Nothing. Hunter waited for a moment, waiting to see what would be the response. After a few minutes without a reply, he shrugged his shoulders, and went back to his mattress. It was time to plan out his next move.

Chapter 26

They walked across a huge lawn and down a slope until they reached the stables. Felicia pushed open the doors and walked inside like she owned the place, which, in a way she kind of did.

Despite the open doors on either side, the smell of horses and straw was overwhelming. Jesse glanced at the horses in their stall, reading their names that were written on the doors that held them. Above their heads straw fell from the hay loft as a young man made his way to the ladder to reach them.

In his dark blue jeans, cowboy boots, and tan and black checkered shirt, he looked very inch the cowboy. His hazel eyes held a gleam in them, like he had just planned something mischievous. He patted a horse absentmindedly, immediately getting a response from the horse, who begged for attention. It was almost as if they spoke the same language, without having to speak a word.

"Felicia," he nodded his head respectfully, "What can I do for you?" he asked as he pushed his sandy brown hair out of his face.

"I need Star, Snow, Missy, and Thunder," Felicia said.

"Yes, ma'am," he went to get them, coming back in a startling short amount of time with four saddled and bridled horses.

Felicia nodded her thanks and took the horses out to the meadow.

"Do any of you know how to ride a horse?" Felicia asked.

"I've ridden a few times, at my uncle's house," Saralee said, her parents had made sure she went to her uncle's house every summer to help him on his ranch.

Jordan and Jesse shook their heads. They hadn't even been this close to a horse before, let alone rode one.

"Okay, start on the left side. Put your left foot in the stirrup, one hand should have the reins and the horn of the saddle, the other at the end of it. Push off with your right foot and swing your leg over and you've just gotten on your horse," she said, demonstrating as she explained the procedure, "Saralee, you may have a little trouble, since your leg is in a cast, but the rest of you should do fine."

Getting off her horse, she watched as the others tried to mount their steeds. They found it wasn't as easy as Felicia had made it look. Even amongst the cumbersome cast, Saralee was the first to figure out how to get on her horse. After about fifteen minutes, Jesse and Jordan too managed to get on their horses, looking more like sacks of potatoes being thrown onto the horses' back than a human riding a horse.

Once they were all on their horses, Felicia said, "Okay, now with your heels, kick him, and follow me."

After a few minutes of leisurely walking, Felicia suddenly came to a stop.

"That was to help you get the hang of being on the horse and being in control of the horse, but if you are in a battle, you won't ever be going at that pace unless you want to get killed. Let's start with a trot and then work our way up to a gallop and then a full run. Remember, move with the horse," she went off on a trot, leaving the rest of them to follow her pace.

The mid afternoon sun was creating an overwhelming heat by the time they finally got back to the stables. All but Felicia practically fell off their horses with exhaustion. They lead their horses tiredly back to the stables, welcoming the surprisingly cool air inside.

"How was the riding lesson?" the stable boy asked, a grin on his face and a gleam in his eye.

He could see that all but Felicia looked about ready to collapse from exhaustion, and was finding it rather amusing. He loved the looks of new riders after their first ride.

"Tiring," Saralee said, her leg was throbbing, and it could be seen on her face.

"Extremely," Jesse said, looking about ready to curl up in the stall and sleep.

"Fine," Jordan said, he didn't like the fact that the stable boy seemed to be laughing at them.

"You'll get used to it," the stable boy encouraged, "Everybody does, with practice."

Horses were easy. He understood them. They were a lot easier to understand than humans most of the time.

"We don't have a lot of time," Felicia said, knowing that she was about to ask the stable boy to go against his normal stable rules, "Would you mind taking care of the horses, Carl?"

Carl, the stable boy, eyed Felicia sternly. She knew the rules better than anyone. If a person wanted to ride a horse, they should take care of the horse. You respect the horse, the horse will respect you. Taking care of them built a trust and a respect that was essential in horseback riding. If you wanted to commit to riding a horse, you had to commit to the care as well.

The two of them stared each other down while the trio looked on, unsure of what they should do in this situation. Unsure of really what was going on. Shouldn't this Carl dude be rushing off to do Felicia's bidding? True, he didn't look much older than Felicia, but she was still the daughter of Mara. That should have brought with her some leverage.

After a few minutes of this stare down, Carl relented, realizing the time crunch they were in. He nodded. As he relented, Felicia breathed a sigh of relief, and nodded her head as well, confirming that she knew that this was the only time she could get away with this request. Then, Felicia quickly ushered the group out of Carl's domain before he could change his mind.

They walked into an area encircled by a white fence. Felicia led them to a shed in one corner. The doors swung open, showing off all kinds of weapons. Weapons the trio had only heard of in stories, or seen on TV, still others they hadn't even heard about, much less know how to use. There were enough weapons there to arm and entire army and then some.

"We'll start with crossbows," Felicia said, choosing an assortment of them and walking out of the shed with them in her arms.

They had just gotten to the crossbow range when James, the trainer, sauntered up to them. His black hair was slicked back, and his brown eyes eyed the trio, assessing them.

"Felicia, nice to see you again," he said, his voice sounded different than the others, like he came from somewhere else, but they couldn't figure out where.

"James, I'm so glad to see you," the relief evident in Felicia's voice, "I'd like you to meet Jordan, Saralee, and Jesse," she pointed to each of them as their names were spoken.

"Nice to meet y'all," he said, shaking each of their hands in turn.

"Would you mind teaching them how to fight?" she asked.

She dreaded teaching. She could make do, especially if it was one on one, but in a group larger than her and pupil, she felt at an utter loss as to what to do. James was perfect for it. He had taught both her and Hunter everything that they knew. Teaching came as naturally to him as breathing. If anyone could teach them what they needed to know in their short time frame, it would be James.

"Of course," his eyes danced.

He loved teaching, and had been deprived of the privilege for too long. He would relish this.

"Wait," Saralee said, "I thought you were going to train us."

Saralee wanted Felicia there, she didn't understand why, but she felt this odd connection to Felicia, and wanted her to be the one to do the training.

"I thought I would too," Felicia confirmed, "But James is our trainer, so he'll do the training."

"Why, can't you fight?" Jordan asked.

"Yes, I know how to fight. But a teacher, I am not," she admitted as she walked away.

"Don't give her too much trouble," James assured them, "She's wicked when it comes to fighting. She's one of the best. No one can quite decide if she or Hunter is the better fighter," James assured them of her talent, "However, while she is better than Hunter is when it comes to teaching, she still struggles teaching others what she knows. That's where I come in," he said with a cocky grin.

Felicia shook her head. She had to admit James balanced Hunter out, they were an odd pair, to be sure, but they had the perfect friendship. She didn't envy the person who would have to tell James about the Hunter situation. He could be told later, right now, the trio needed a teacher, and he needed to focus.

Chapter 27

In a need to boil out the excess energy that her anger caused to surge through her veins, Flara paced up and down her throne room. She punched her right hand with her left hand, and, using her left hand, she squeezed her right hand. As she took deep breaths, she rubbed her hand over and over again.

"Blackheart!" she called out once she had calmed down enough to face people.

"Yes ma'am," he said as he walked in and stepped in front of her.

"Put Hunter in the water room of the chamber."

His eyes widened in surprise, "Yes ma'am," he nodded, and still reeling from his orders, he headed down to the dungeon to get Hunter.

At the sound of his cell door opening, Hunter sat up, his shoulders straight, ready to fight.

"Get up," Blackheart growled.

"Don't tell me what to do," Hunter said, refusing to get to his feet.

He had never taken orders from anyone, and he certainly wasn't about to start with a person like Blackheart.

Blackheart pulled Hunter up by his collar and slapped handcuffs on his wrists. He dragged Hunter down to the chamber. Blackheart quickly shoved him through the door that led to the water chamber.

The room was aptly named. A throne overlooked a huge tub of water in the middle of the room. Hunter was just about to assess the chains hanging from the ceiling when the door opened and Flara walked in with Rickstin following behind her.

Rickstin had gained some more trust for getting Hunter to Flara, and had been allowed to sit in and help with the torture, adding a jaunt in his step. With a nod from Flara, Rickstin picked Hunter up by the back of his neck and threw him into the waiting tub of water.

Hunter swam back to the surface, trying to catch his breath and get over the shock of the freezing cold water. Just as he had caught his breath, he was shoved under again. He continued that cycle of barely getting to breathe before getting pushed down once again. Finally, after ten to fifteen minutes of such practice, Hunter was pulled out of the water and thrown none too gently to the ground.

His body had unconsciously started shivering, trying to regain the body heat that had fled as he stayed too long in too cold water. The room did nothing to help warm him, in fact, it seemed to have dropped several degrees since he had been put into the water.

Flara smiled. It wasn't much, but it was nice to be able to see Hunter's broken body, shivering so hard his teeth were actually beginning to chatter. It was enough, for her, at least for right now.

Chapter 28

To the great relief of the trio, James finally called for a rap up of the day's lessons. Jesse pretended to fall down dead of exhaustion as James began to gather up the weapons. The others smiled weakly at her attempted humor.

"I'm not moving," Jesse yawned tiredly.

"I think you'll want to," James said, "There's food up at the castle."

"Food?" all of their eyes lit up at the thought.

They hadn't stopped for lunch, and were going on what they had eaten for breakfast, and the little bits of jerky that they had managed to eat in between their lessons.

"It's getting late and you all must be extremely tired, so I'll let you guys go," James said, locking up the shed, "Do you know the way back?"

"I think we can manage," Jordan responded.

"Are you sure?" he raised his eyebrow, glancing over at Saralee subtly, "I'd be happy to escort you back."

"We'd love your help back," Saralee chimed in before anyone else had a chance to turn him down again.

James nodded and happily escorted them back to Mara's throne room. After a long day of training, the trip back was slow going.

"I've come to return your guests," James said, with an exaggerated bow toward Mara.

"Thank you James," she smiled, nodding her head in acknowledgement.

It was a running gag they had going. James was one of the few people who was allowed to get away with such antics.

"You guys must be hungry and tired. I've kept some dinner warm for you and had a cool bath drawn up for you. Everything is ready," Mara turned, and spoke to the trio.

They simply nodded their heads, and a servant led them to the kitchen and on to their reward for such hard work.

"So?" Mara quirked her eyebrow, "How were they?"

James was just about to give her an answer to her inquiry when Felicia floated in.

"Oh, sorry," she said softly, "I didn't mean to interrupt you two," she was just about to close the door and head back up to her room when her mother stopped her.

"No, no come in. Then I'll only have to ask once," Mara waved her in.

"Okay," Felicia closed the door behind her and walked forward.

"Now, how did they do today?"

"Jesse, after some trouble actually getting on the horse, took to it like a fish to water. She's a natural. Saralee was just as good, but had some difficulty when we were going too fast, but that could be because of her leg. Jordan was terrible. He can get on one, but actually doing anything while on a horse, well," she sighed, "That was something you just have to see to believe, it was terrible."

Felicia nodded to James at the end, letting him know it was his turn.

"I did an introduction and tutorial on fighting skills. Kind of getting them used to the basics of it all, and see where their skills lied and what to focus more attention on. Jordan was wonderful when it came to fighting. I could give him anything and after a little practice he would excel at it. Saralee was alright. She did have trouble with the crossbow and the knife, but you give her a bow and arrow or a sword, she's a whiz. Jesse had a problem with all the weapons, but she's good at hiding and diverting people so someone else can come up on an attack from behind," James said.

"So what do you think of them?" Mara asked, when he had finished.

"They could be real assets to us," Felicia said.

"You think they're the ones?" James asked, eyeing the two of them.

The oracle had told them that Janette would return to them someday, bringing with her siblings that would help them. They could be the turning point for the war against Flara.

"I'll have to contact Leana and Pete before I know anything for sure," Mara replied, not wanting to jump the gun, "Now go," she waved the two of them out, she had things she needed to do.

James and Felicia walked out of the room, their minds whirling. Could they really have found her? She did kind of look like Hunter. Had Janette finally found her way home?

Chapter 29

Hunter had no control. He had no control of his limbs, that were shaking furiously, as if he was being shocked, and the electricity was causing his body to spasm like a fish out of water. He had no control of his mind either. It jumped from thought to thought, place to place. His mind was swimming in a river of painful and confusing memories. However, no matter how far it moved, no matter which direction it flowed, it always somehow made its way back to the night of the fire.

The memories came toward him like a hungry monster, destroying everything that it could get its hands on. He could feel the memory monster coming closer, so close that Hunter could feel the burning in his lungs that that memory always brought with it. The memory was so real, so tangible that he could actually feel the oxygen fleeing. His eyes began to sting with the smoke, just as they had that night. There was no air. He was confused. He wanted to yell out in anger and pain.

As he struggled with the memories, he couldn't help but wish that he had been able to make it through the portal. Or, if he had to do what he did, sacrifice himself for the others, that at least he wished that he could be on his prickly mattress in his cell upstairs. At least there was some kind of cushion to ease his weary bones.

"He is ready," Flara said to Blackheart.

"Yes ma'am," he nodded, picking Hunter up like he weighed less than a sack of potatoes.

Hunter felt himself being lifted off the cold floor. Although he felt like his limbs were made of cement, he found himself floating through the air, still shaking, giving the illusion of a magician giving an interpretive dance of a spasmodic turkey.

"Take him to the interrogation room."

He continued to float in the air, moving toward the interrogation room. All too soon, Hunter found himself falling, until he reached a hard chair. He tried to force his eyes to focus, but the task was Herculean in nature, and was beyond his capabilities.

"What are you thinking of?" Flara's voice popped into his head.

The voice grated on his nerves, causing Hunter to tighten.

"Tell me what you see," she pressed gently, but urgently, firmly, as she reached out and played with his hair, like a mother does with their small child.

"Fire, smoke, destruction," the words came out as if Hunter was in a trance. His voice sounded foreign and faraway to his own ears. Still, he swam through the memories, "And you," he tried to force emotion into his voice, but was unable to do so, "You caused it," his voice was so quiet, it was hardly there at all.

He had no control. He didn't really want to talk, but couldn't seem to get his voice to obey him. The trance he seemed to be in just forced the words out of his mouth unconsciously.

"Was it really me?" that voice, that grating voice, once again hit his ears, "Mara was there too. How do you know it was me who caused it?"

As the voice spoke to him, the figure in his mind began to glitch out. The figure in the midst of the smoke that originally looked like Flara, suddenly began to look like Mara. He shook his head slightly, and it was back to Flara. Back and forth it went, until he couldn't tell if it was supposed to be Flara or Mara that he was looking at.

"How do you know that?" the voice urged, "Maybe Mara did

all of this. You were young. She could have told you anything and you would have believed her."

"No," Hunter shook his head.

"I'm the victim here," Flara said, barely keeping her voice from shaking with emotion.

"No," Hunter shook his head as the figure in his head glitched back and forth harder and faster.

"How do I get to the portal? What are Mara's plans? What is she planning?" the voice became less lilting, less maternal, and more demanding, pushing him.

"No," he said, "You took them."

"Did I?" she asked innocently, dialing back her voice once again.

Hunter looked cross eyed at her, unable to focus his eyes on her. Flara had to have done it. His whole life would have been a lie if she hadn't. He knew the truth. However, his mind was beginning to pound as it raced around in circles, making it difficult for him to recognize what was true.

"Mara was there too. She planned it all. She made me look bad. I trusted her, and she used me. I'm just trying to save what's left of your little family. I want to protect you," the maternal tone in Flara's voice had once again returned, and she was once again lovingly stroking his hair.

Hunter's head began to fall as it got heavier and heavier with the struggle between trying to figure out the truth from the lies. His eyes began to roll around in his head, trying to find an escape. Flara smiled. He was cracking. As his head met his chest, Flara nodded toward Blackheart.

Without any need for words, Blackheart swooped Hunter up into his arms, carrying him as gently as a sleeping child. As he was laid to rest on his mat, his eyes rolled all the way back, as his body gave up the fight and he lost touch of reality.

Chapter 30

Jesse's body revolted at even the thought of moving it. Still, she knew she didn't have a choice. Taking a deep breath, she forced herself out of her bed. Moving gingerly, she put on the clothes that were closest to her, which happened to be a pair of light grey sweatpants and a white t-shirt. All her energy drained from her, she simply threw her hair into a ponytail to get it out of her face. She took a glance at herself in the mirror and frowned as she noticed how much she looked like an invalid.

Boom. Boom. Boom. Saralee listened to the sound of her heart, noticing that the throbbing in her leg was throbbing in time with the sound of her heartbeat. She wanted to pamper herself. She wanted to lounge around all day. But she couldn't. She couldn't afford to take a day off. She had to get started. Before she could talk herself out of it, she forced herself out of bed and pulled on some jogging clothes and headed to the kitchen, hoping that she'd find something to eat so that she could take care of the pain in her leg.

As normal, Jordan woke in a bad mood. He didn't do mornings, and most people knew to stay as far away as possible from him for at least two hours after he had woken up. Today was no different. In fact, it might have been worse.

"Good morning," Felicia said cheerily, as the group made their way into the kitchen.

Unlike Jordan, Felicia loved mornings. She loved getting up before the sun, and watching the sky change colors as the sun greeted the earth. Mornings brought with it promises and hope. The morning was full of potential. So much could be done, and she thrived on that feeling.

"Good morning," Jesse said, taking an apple from the bowl on the table and cutting into it.

"Did you sleep well?" Mara asked, sitting at the end of the table.

She was glancing at some papers in her hands, and had barely looked up as they walked into the room.

"Slept beautifully," Saralee replied, "It was the waking up that was the hard part," she joked.

They ate in silence, each too tired and too involved in their own thoughts to make any chitchat.

"You guys ready for more training?" Cara asked after their breakfast was over.

"As ready as I'll ever be," Jesse said, not really joking.

"You'll be working in the rink today," Mara told them as she rang the bell to have their breakfast plates taken away.

"What about horseback riding?" Jesse asked, trying not to sound too much like a child in her request, but she had really wanted to get in another horseback lesson.

"If you have time after today's lesson, then you can do some more riding, if not, we'll get to it another day," Felicia commented.

"If I recall correctly, we don't have much longer before the portal can be opened again, and we can be attacked," Jordan said, going over things he had been told, his mind naturally going into planning mode, "We aren't ready to fight if something comes in to attack us," plans were beginning to formulate in his head as he tried to come up with ideas for evacuation, or a head on fight, trying to calculate which risk he should take and what outcomes could possibly come with it.

"Flara won't jump into this war. She'll take some time. She'll assemble an army, build her forces before she attacks. She's too much of a planner. She isn't going to do something rash, it's always well thought through," Cara explained, trying to ease Jordan's anxieties.

"What if she does?" Jordan asked, not willing to be appeased by something like these meaningless words.

He knew all too well that people didn't always act the way you thought they should. Motivations changed, and behaviors did too, causing you to realize you didn't know someone as well as you thought you did. He wasn't going to allow himself to be duped yet again.

"We do have an army if it comes to that," Mara explained calmly.

"And you have time before the portal can be opened again to get ready," Felicia said, taking a different but similar approach than Cara had, but her consolations fell flat, alleviating none of the situation, "Okay," she said, dragging out the word when she was met with silence, "I'll take you guys down to the rink."

Chapter 31

"**N**ot my fault, I'm the victim," Hunter heard the words over and over again in his head as his mind replayed that night over and over again.

The room had seemed large at the time, but then again, he had been a child, everything had felt large. In reality, the room had probably been fairly small. No bigger than the living room in Cara's cottage. Hunter had been sitting on the worn out brown rug in front of the fire, playing with some wooden toys. His mother had been sitting nearby, rocking his sister to sleep in the cherry wood rocking chair that Pete and Leana had given to her as a present when he had been born.

Hunter remembered sharing his truck with Felicia, and glancing up at his father, who had smiled down approvingly at the sight. He remembered feeling so proud of himself at that moment. They were all laughing, and having a great time. There was no clue that his entire life was about to be turned upside-down.

In a blink of an eye, the door of the cottage flew open. A man staggered in. He was covered from head to foot in soot. His left arm was pressed up against his stomach to stem off the bleeding that was coming from a wound. It was a pointless endeavor. Too much damage had been done. Too much blood had been lost. His end was near.

"The town, it's burning," the man gasped, "They're destroying everything," the last of the man's strength ebbed out of him, and he fell to the ground, never to move again.

Mara hurried toward the man's dead body and placed a hand at his neck, checking for a pulse, even though she knew that it was another pointless endeavor. He was gone. Tears rushed to her eyes, but she refused to let them fall. Instead, she pursed her lips together tightly.

Not knowing what was going on, Hunter and Felicia had toddled over to the body and began to try to get the man to play.

"Papa," Felicia said, patting his shoulder, trying to get him to sit up and grab her, and tickle her, "Papa," she said more forcefully, when the first time elicited no response.

Cara had moved quickly, swooping Felicia into her arms and walking away from Felicia's father. Coming out of his stupor, Hunter's father did the same with Hunter. Hunter could still feel the tickling of his father's black-beard. He could still smell the smell of the outdoors that seemed to cling to his father's body. He could still recall how his father's green eyes twinkled with delight in everything his son did. He was truly the apple of his father's eye, even though Janette had everyone else, including his father, wrapped around her little finger, unable to do no wrong.

With each of the kids safely in an adult's arms, the group sprinted for the portal. They had to get the kids to safety. They never made it. Halfway to the entrance, Hunter's father had realized it was an exercise in futility. He stopped abruptly, causing Pete to stop as well. No words had to be spoken. Hunter's father simply passed his son over to Pete.

Hunter remembered thinking how different Pete looked compared to his father, with a clean shaven baby face instead of a face with whiskers, deep blue eyes instead of green, that didn't seem to twinkle nearly as much as his father's did.

Hunter cocked his head to the side, confused at the transition. He was even more confused when his mother passed Janette over to Leanna. Hunter fought to be turned loose. Pete gratefully placed the squirming child down.

"Be a good boy," Hunter's father said, kneeling down in front of his son and placing a heavy, but loving hand on Hunter's shoulder, "Take care of your sister."

Still confused, Hunter found his hand being taken up by Pete as he was led forward, leaving his parents to fall further and further behind.

He stared at his parents, and while he did so, he saw his father fall to the ground, an arrow in his back. The shock of his father falling like his uncle had, caused Hunter to lose hold of Pete's hand. As he stared, he saw his mother get taken away by someone he later learned was called Mintus.

He remembered tears falling down his face. He cried, for his parents, at being lost, tired, and confused. As he cried the smoke burned his eyes and lungs, but he didn't move. He didn't know where to go. At some point, a beautiful lady swooped him into her arms and took him to Mara.

He remembered being taken to the castle, and told to play with his cousin. For what seemed like an eternity to him, he was forced to stay with his cousin, under the watchful eye of Carl's mother. Finally, Mara was taking him to a little cottage. Cara stepped out of the cottage with a smile, and the two women kneeled down beside him.

"This is Cara," Mara said, "You know Cara," Hunter nodded. He knew Cara. He had spent time with her. She often watched him when his parents couldn't, "She's going to be your new mommy."

"No," he said in the defiant way only a two year old could pull off.

"She was a friend of your parents, and they want you to go with her, okay?"

Hunter sulked but in the end, he allowed Cara to lead him

inside. True to Mara's words, Cara had taken him in, taken care of him, and had in fact become his new mommy.

Hunter woke in a cold sweat as the words 'I'm the victim,' rang through his head. Those three little words had the power to make him question everything he remembered about that night.

His carefully managed memories of that night were suddenly breaking out of their boxes, and rushing over him, taking over his waking hours. The memories were making his life a living nightmare, one that there was no escape from.

"Mara was there. It was her fault. She blamed me. I'm the victim," continued to ring through his head.

It couldn't be possible. No, he couldn't believe it. If that was true, his entire existence was a lie. Everything he believed, everything he knew, was a lie. No, he couldn't accept that.

"No," he shouted. He kicked at the cement wall. When that didn't help, he started using his fists to pound it.

He didn't know what he was trying to accomplish with his attack of the wall. All he knew was that helped him think, and he needed all the help he could at the moment.

There was the sound of movement on the other side of the wall and the note came back to him. Hunter bent over and read it.

Are you okay?

Ya, I'm fine.

What were you shouting for?

Nothing.

Want to discuss it?

No.

Is it because of what happened in the chamber?

How do you know about that?

The only thing downstairs is that chamber. I saw them take you down and carry you back up.

Oh. No, I'm good.

I'm here. If you need to talk.

Hunter didn't even bother to respond. He didn't want to talk.

Even if he had wanted, his mind hurt too much to even begin to try to disentangle everything enough to be able to talk about it to someone else and even hope to make sense. This was something that he'd have to figure out alone, which was exactly what he wanted, to be alone.

It was years ago, but right now, he felt very much like the little boy who had witnessed his parent's die before his eyes. Yet, unlike that little boy, he couldn't cry. There was no one there to take care of him. This time, he was truly alone.

Chapter 32

"**Y**ou guys have done great," James cheered them on as they sat on the grass eating the lunch that had been sent out to them.

"Thanks," Jesse yawned, leaning her back against the fence of the rink.

"Alright, now that I've seen what your strengths and weaknesses are, we can start to do more personalized training," James said, finishing off the apple he was eating and standing up.

"Now?" Jesse inquired.

"Now," he confirmed with a firm nod, "Come on, get up!" he clapped his hands together. He was in no-nonsense, teacher mode, "We need to get a move on."

While Jesse and Saralee got to their feet in an exhausted stupor, Jordan jumped to his feet with excitement coursing through his veins. Saralee grimaced as a hot, searing pain flew up her leg. She tried to remain stoic, but a small gasp escaped her mouth.

"Here, take this," James pulled out a bottle of pills from the basket that held their lunches, and handed it over to her, "It should help with the pain in your leg."

While James was taking care of Saralee, Jordan had run to the shed. He tried to keep himself from pacing back and forth with the anticipation he felt. James smiled. He handed Saralee and Jesse some weapons first before turning toward Jordan.

"I think I'll give you a sword and crossbow," James pulled each one out and handed them to Jordan.

When they had their weapons in their hands, Felicia walked into the arena, dressed for training. With a nod, James assigned Felicia to Jordan. He needed very little prompting, and would be good practice for him. Saralee and Jesse needed more attention. He'd handle them.

"Let's take a short break and get some rest before we continue," James said, as the afternoon sun beat down on them relentlessly. The heat sapped them all of any strength they might have after their lunches.

As they sat down to rest, James threw some water bottles to each of them. The trio tore into their water enthusiastically. They hardly stopped to breathe until all the water was gone.

"How are they doing?" Felicia whispered, as she and James watched them take their break.

"Remarkably well," James confirmed, "I have perfect faith that they'll do well when the time comes," his cockiness slipped out once again.

Felicia noticed the gleam of pride in his eyes as he watched his pupils.

"Great," she said, "Well, you guys must be exhausted," Felicia turned her attention to the trio, "You guys have done great. Why don't we take a horseback ride and then we can take the rest of the afternoon off?"

"Great," Jesse smiled.

"Okay," Saralee said with less enthusiasm.

Getting the afternoon off did sound nice, but the horseback riding didn't. She really just wanted to rest her leg. However, if a forced horseback ride got her that, she'd take it.

"I guess," Jordan said, rather reluctantly.

The horses had made him feel like a fool. They didn't make sense, and he couldn't seem to get a handle on them. He would much rather get a few more hours of practice in than ever get on another horse.

Carl was just finishing up cleaning the stalls when the four of them walked into the stables.

"Same horses?" he asked, he didn't even look up from cleaning his tools when they walked in.

"Yes," Felicia confirmed.

Carl nodded, and walked off to get the horses. When he brought them out, Jordan blanked. The horses didn't have saddles or bridles on. How were they supposed to ride if they didn't have saddles and bridles?

Felicia nodded. She understood perfectly. The stables were Carl's domain, and he had rules that must be followed. He had allowed it once. She knew better than to expect or even ask for it, a second time.

Carl leaned up against the frame of the barn door as Felicia taught the trio how to saddle and bridle their horses. He noticed how well Jesse took to it. She was a natural. She had managed to get her horse saddles and bridles on the first try, and was now trying to help Jordan get the hang of it. No matter how hard he tried, he couldn't quite grasp the concept.

Carl couldn't help a smile that spread across his face as he watched the twins work together. She was so patient with him, and he was getting so frustrated at how incapable he seemed at taking care of the horses.

The two of them certainly made an interesting team. They balanced each other out.

Chapter 33

As the days passed, so did Hunter's nightmares. His mind no longer found the need to plague him with memories. The confusion began to fade. He knew what he knew. He knew the truth, and no longer had to question his memories.

Flara had been lying to him. She had been praying on his weakened state of mind. She had manipulated it so that he would be confused, so that he would trust her.

As his mind started coming back to him, he found his strength was willing to return as well. With his mind clear, he began to get back to his planning. It was much easier when his mind wasn't in a haze and full of cloudiness.

The days dragged on. Hunter had long lost count of his imprisonment. It didn't seem to matter all that much anyway. Days faded into each other, each one bringing its own set of torment. They'd allow him to regain some composure only to be taken down into a deeper sense of pain.

The only way of escape was death or to give in, which was its own kind of death.

Chapter 34

Mara took a deep breath to steady herself. It was impossible. It couldn't be, not after all these years, after all the planning they had gone through. She knew it shouldn't surprise her, after all, their plan had fallen apart from the very beginning.

Hunter's parents should have made it. Leana and Pete were only supposed to take Hunter and Janette temporarily. When that no longer a possibility, at least the two of them were supposed to be raised together. Hunter should have been raised with his sister, not as an only child, but knowing that he wasn't. That was torment. It was torture, always knowing that there was a missing piece in his heart. He shouldn't have grown up feeling like a failure for failing to keep his sister safe, for not even knowing where she was.

All of it was wrong. The only thing right was Leana and Pete taking Janette and changing her name so that not even Mara knew what it was. It was a way to protect the child. And now all of that was gone.

Felicia stepped into the room, and noticed her mother's distress right away. Mara was never able to hide anything from Felicia, not since the day she had seen her father die. Mara had lost it that day. She couldn't have made it through if it hadn't been for Felicia and Cara pushing her forward. Felicia became her mother's most trusted confidante and advisor, keeping away the pain that that night had brought with it, a pain that never seemed to end.

"What is it?" she asked, rushing to her mother's side, and lowering her into her throne.

In their normal pattern, Felicia took Mara's hands and began to rub it gently, releasing the tension that caused Mara's hands to ball up into fists.

"I just got in contact with Leana," Mara's voice was barely above a whisper.

She still couldn't believe it. She was reeling. She hadn't felt this confused and terrible since the night of the intrusion.

"She's not with them, is she?" Felicia guessed the reason for her mother's distress.

"No, she's been gone for over a month," Mara confirmed, even though it didn't need to be confirmed.

"Is she?" started Felicia, unable to fully form the question.

"Yes," Mara nodded numbly, "It's incredible. After all these years with hardly any contact with them, and absolutely none with her, and now this? Now she's here? It's simply incredible."

"Is she to be told?"

"No," Mara shook her head, "At least not yet. We can't tell her. It can't come from us. It needs to come from Leana and Pete. She needs to be told by the people she knows and trusts, the people who raised her."

"Do you think Hunter knew?"

"I don't know," Mara shrugged.

He had always been a strange child. He had seen things no one else saw, he could feel things that no one else could. It was like he had a sixth sense, a sense that let him know things that he couldn't possibly know.

"Who knows? Who knows what he remembers, what he knows? He doesn't talk about that night. He doesn't talk about her. Who knows what he knew before he was taken?"

"I guess the next question is, does Flara know who she is?"

"Unfortunately yes," Mara's fingers began to curl again, despite Felicia's rubbing.

"What do we do now?"

"Nothing. We keep on doing what we've been doing, at least until I can arrange for safe transportation of Leana and Pete. Once they get here, we can let them tell her the story, and go from there."

The two of them sat in silence. Felicia rubbed Mara's hands, more out of reflex, than actual realization of what she was doing.

A knock on the door made them both jump. Mara quickly composed herself, straightening herself out, and giving herself the air of confidence that she always held about her. She was acting queen, and she would act like it even if it killed her. Felicia let go of her mother's hand and stood up as well and dusted off her training outfit. She stood, straight, squaring her shoulders and trying to look as regal as her mother did.

"Come in," Mara called out, after confirming that both of them were looking presentable.

As Saralee stepped into the room she could feel the nervousness and confusion that was permeating the air. It settled on her like a ton of bricks, making it difficult to breathe.

"Am I interrupting something?" she asked, looking between the two of them trying to get a handle on what had happened and what was going on that would cause such an intense emotion.

"Not at all," Mara said calmly, "Can we help you?"

Felicia glanced over at her mother. It never ceased to impress Felicia how quickly her mother was able to step into the role of leader; of how quickly she could become the queen again. It was amazing how she was able to compose herself and not allow people to see how shaken up she was.

There was only one time that Mara had allowed her emotions to get the better of her. Only one time where Mara hadn't been able to keep composed, and others were allowed to see what she was feeling. It was a long time ago. It was the day Felicia's father, Mara's husband, died. That night ended a lot of innocence, and turned a lot of lives upside down. That was the last time Mara had allowed herself to lose her composure.

"Yes," Saralee nodded, "At least, I hope you can," she added with a little less certainty.

"Well?" Mara prodded gently, trying to get Saralee to the point. "What's going on here?"

"What do you mean?"

"Why are we here? Why do we need to be here? What makes us so important to you? How do we fit into this situation? What exactly is the situation? I want some answers."

"You are here because you want to be here, because someone you trusted brought you here. We need you to help us destroy Flara. I can't go into all the details of WHY or HOW, but in time, you'll learn what is so important," Mara explained.

She stood, walked to Saralee and put her arms around Saralee's shoulders, before leading her to the door before Saralee could ask any more questions.

"Maybe you should take a walk, it'll clear your head."

Saralee allowed herself to be led out of the room, but this was far from over. She would figure out what was going on.

Chapter 35

Hunter blinked at the brightness of the outside world as he was marched into the sunlight. As they continued their march, Hunter took deep breaths, as if trying to make up for all the time that he had been imprisoned; of all the times he hadn't been able to really breathe. Blackheart and Rickstin stood on either side of him to make sure he didn't try to run away again.

As they waited in the sunlight, Hunter moved his hands down to where Rickstin held his knife against Hunter's back. Slowly, with calculated movements, so as not to alert the two of them to what he was doing, Hunter cut his bonds. As Hunter's hands broke free, he allowed his hands to meet Blackheart and Rickstin's faces.

While their eyes watered and they tried to regain their bearings, Hunter made a run for it. He ran past people working, fighting off anyone who tried to stop him. He made it halfway across the fort when Flara's soldiers started pouring out from all over. He wouldn't have been surprised if he actually saw them coming up from the ground. He put in another burst of speed, fought harder, ran faster, until he felt like he was almost flying his feet were going so fast. But it was in vain. There were too many of them, too close together. He couldn't beat them all, he couldn't outrun them.

He had just gotten past one group of soldiers when another came up from behind him, while others came up from behind and to his sides. Still, he wouldn't give up. He couldn't. Giving up meant death, and he wasn't ready to die. He would make it to the portal. He had to make it. He had to get Mara. He had to tell her what he had found out. He had to know if Janette was safe. His sister's safety was the thing that kept him going. Just thinking about that made him push himself even harder to make it to the portal.

He had almost made it to the gate when he was overcome by soldiers. Even his strong motivations weren't enough to get him through. He had at least ten people for each of his arms and legs. They tackled him, held him down, and no matter how hard he tried to fight them off, they were stronger.

Ten people to each limb, dragged him back to the dungeon where he was once again handed over to Blackheart and Rickstin. The two of them tied Hunter's arms up once again and, with their group of soldiers, they marched him back to cell.

Leaving his hands bound behind his back, Hunter was shoved into his cell. Unable to catch himself from his fall, he fell flat onto his face. His nose snapped, and blood came gushing out of it and the air rushed out of his lungs, making breathing impossible.

He had just managed to catch his breath when his cell door was shoved open and Flara stormed inside. Grabbing his collar, she pulled him to a standing position. Using her free hand, she slapped his face. A large red mark rose on his cheek, a testament of just how hard she had slapped him. As if the abuse he had already faced wasn't enough, she grabbed his hair and pulled it backwards until he was forced to look at her.

"How dare you? I tried to play nice, but you just won't let me, will you? This is it, there will be no more mercy from me. You've pushed me too far and you will pay for it," she let his hair go and pushed him back to the floor.

"Guards! Take him down to the chamber," she stormed off, her black robes billowing behind her.

Two guards Hunter had never seen before, picked him up and

dragged him down the stairs, letting his body slam against each and every step. By the time they reached the bottom, every part of Hunter's body was covered in bruises.

"Pick a room, any room, and put him in there," she said to Blackheart, who had been following behind them.

A wicked grin crossed Blackheart's lips as he plotted his revenge for what Hunter had done. His nose was still throbbing from where Hunter had punched him. He was going to make Hunter beg for release, but they wouldn't give him that pleasure.

Chapter 36

Saralee wandered around the grounds. She needed to vent off some steam, and since her broken leg made her normal running session impossible, she settled for simply hobbling as quickly as she could across the cobblestoned streets.

She was 17 years old. That wasn't a child anymore. None of them were children. They deserved to know what was going on. She knew Mara, Cara, and Felicia were keeping things from her, from them.

The wandering did little to help her organize her thoughts. Only running could do such a thing. Since her normal outlet was taken from her, she decided to allow herself to relax, and soothe her pounding leg with a bubble bath.

She eased herself into the water, letting the warmth calm her nerves and release the tension that had been building up. It wasn't quite as good as a run would have been, but it would be enough, at least for now. She eased even further into the water, letting her mind go blank.

Jordan was having similar problems. He stormed about the mansion. He went into every room in the palace. Here he was, being trained to fight and to ride a stupid horse and they wouldn't tell him why. He wasn't a child. None of them were. Not anymore. Not after everything they had been through. They should be told what was going on. They should at least know why they were there and who these people were.

He toyed around with the thought of going to Mara and demanding an explanation for what was going on. He had already tried to puzzle out what he knew, to fit the pieces together, but it wasn't adding up. He knew he wasn't getting the whole picture. He wanted to yell in frustration.

Instead of hounding Mara, he went out to do some target practice. At least that could be useful. He'd probably get more information, or at least more use out of the practice than he would trying to get anything out of Mara.

He pulled back the string and let the arrow fly. His anger left him with every punch, with every hit of the target, his anger released.

Jesse decided to take a walk down to the stables to clear her head. She wasn't mad, not really. She didn't see any reason to be mad. She was just confused. There was no reason behind what was going on, and that was confusing her. It made her feel useless.

Jesse walked into the stables and up to Midnight's stall and started to gently run her hand over his face.

"He's beautiful, isn't he?" Carl stood up from where he was sitting, leaning against the doorway of the stable.

Jesse jumped and turned around with a hand on her chest. He sauntered over toward her.

"You scared me," she gasped as she caught her breath and her heart stopped pounding.

"Sorry about that," he said sheepishly.

He hadn't truly meant to scare her. He had simply faded in with the background, and hadn't thought about how just talking would affect someone. He was used to animals, and they didn't seem to mind nearly as much.

"It's okay," she smiled, her breath coming back to normal, "And yes," she confirmed, turning back to the horse and resuming her petting, "He is beautiful."

Carl leaned up against the stall again, crossing his arms, not knowing what else to do with his hands, "What brings you out to the stables so late?"

"It's not late," she argued lightly, "It's barely 7:30."

He shrugged, she had a point, "That still doesn't answer my question. What are you doing out here? After all, you went out riding this afternoon."

"Just needed to clear my head is all," she turned her head to look at him, but didn't break her petting.

"What's on your mind?" he asked curiously.

"It's fine. Don't worry about it," she said.

"Come on, tell me," he urged, he was desperate for conversation, "It may help."

"All of this," she made a wide sweeping gesture.

"What's confusing about it?"

"Well, I just don't know, about any of it. Things just kind of happened, and now it's just, I don't know," she didn't know what was confusing, at least not well enough to explain it to someone else.

In her confusion she began to cry. She wiped them away. She hated that she cried for anything. She was mad, there were tears. She was upset, tears. She was happy, tears. It was like her tears had faucets that she couldn't turn off no matter what.

"Sorry," she said.

"It's alright," he said uncertainly. He wasn't quite sure what to do with any of this. His main source of human interaction weren't really criers, and horses, well, they didn't cry, so he never had to deal with tears. He wasn't sure what he was supposed to do with them. He observed her for a moment, and noticed her wiping them away, and assumed that she wanted to get rid of them, so he grabbed a handkerchief from his pocket and handed it to her

"Thank you," she said softly, wiping her face with the handkerchief.

"Better?" he asked, still uncertain if he had done the right thing.

"Ya, much," she smiled weakly.

"It's getting dark," he glanced outside, "I'll escort you back to the house," he offered.

"That's not necessary," she too turned to look at the darkening sky, "You have work to do. I'll be okay."

"I have to go up anyway," he shrugged, "And besides, Mara would be pretty upset if you end up getting lost."

It was a quiet jaunt back up to the castle. Unsure of whether Jesse wanted to speak more, Carl let himself swallow the questions he had, and simply walked next to her in silence. Jesse was grateful for the silence. She liked having someone walking beside her without feeling the need to make small talk just to keep the silence at bay.

"Good night," she said, outside the throne room.

"Good night," he smiled, "And hey," he said, "It'll be okay. Everything will look better in the morning."

Chapter 37

With a welt raising on his back, Hunter curled up on his side on his mattress. There were bruises all over his body, making him look like a purple monster rather than a human. His chapped lips were bleeding, mixing with the blood that was still on his face from his broken nose. His right eye was almost completely swollen shut and impossible to see anything out of.

He winced and grabbed at his ribs, most of which were broken, as he tried to sit up. Taking small breaths so as not to cause any more pain than necessary, he forced himself to slide across his cell to get to his food. It stuck in his throat, making it hurt to swallow, but he forced himself to eat the whole plate. He needed his strength.

How are you today?

The notes had become a daily ritual. Every morning before he was taken downstairs, and every afternoon when he was brought back, there they were, waiting for him. Oddly enough, they helped Hunter cling to reality, made withstanding torture easier.

I've seen better days, but it's better than it was yesterday.

Good, glad to hear it. You need to stop egging her on. Don't give her any more reason to hurt you. You need to stop all this foolishness.

You want me to give in to her? To give up?

No, that wasn't what I was saying. I'm saying don't make it harder on yourself. It's her game.

Hunter breathed, wincing as he did so. The notewriter was right. It was Flara's game, but that didn't mean she'd have to win. He barely had enough time to push the note back through the hole before Blackheart stormed in and dragged him down the stairs for his daily ritual of torture.

Hunter immediately noticed the chair sitting in the middle of the room, he was shocked when he was shoved into it. Normally he was forced to try and keep himself in a kneeling position with his hands tied behind his back. He glanced curiously around the room. Being allowed to sit, in a chair, without binds, it was like being treated like a king.

"Join me, and all of this can end," Flara said, walking in circles around Hunter's seat.

As he recalled his days here, joining her and ending everything, certainly sounded appealing. No more pain. It was tempting. All he had to do was give up. All he had to do was do what she told him to. That was it, then he could be free, he wouldn't have to deal with any pain. Glancing around the room, he started to wonder just what he was fighting for.

Chapter 38

Cara was sitting on top of Mara's cherry wood desk in the middle of the wall on the opposite side of the four poster queen size bed in Mara's bedroom, while Mara curled herself on the bench at the foot of the bed, leaning against the bed to prop herself up.

"When will they get here?" Cara asked.

"They'll be here late Friday afternoon," Mara played with the fringe on a pillow.

"When are you going to tell her? Will the rest of them be told too?"

"I don't know when or how they're going to tell her. That's up to them. Once she is told, it'll be up to her to decide if she wants to tell the others or not, or what she wants told, and to whom."

Cara nodded. The idea of Leana and Pete coming back to their little village sent the two of them recalling old memories. Skirting around the memory of that night, Mara and Cara spoke of their memories. They spent that night living in the past.

The next morning Saralee and Jesse were talking in Saralee's room when there was a knock on the door and Cara poked her head in.

"Hey," Cara said.

"Hey, what's up?" Saralee asked, sitting cross-legged on her bed.

"I have a surprise for you," she opened the door to show two people.

"Mom! Dad!" Saralee said, shocked.

She jumped off her bed and hurried toward the door, as quickly as her leg would allow.

"Hey honey," Leana said.

"Darling," Pete said, embracing them all.

The three of them pushed inside, and Cara closed the door in order to give them some privacy.

"We have something to tell you," her father said, after they had finished their hugs.

While he wanted to continue to hang onto this girl he had called his daughter for so long, it was much better to just get right to the point of why they were here. Jesse looked at the group. It was an intimate, family moment, and Jesse was feeling like an intruder. She got to her feet and began to skirt around the edges of the room toward the door.

"I'm going to leave," Jesse said, gesturing toward the door.

She hadn't thought that any of them could hear her, but Saralee had noticed the entire situation with Jesse.

"No, you can stay," Saralee said, motioning her to stay put.

"Are you sure?" Jesse asked, still edging toward the door.

"It is something pretty personal," her mother said, agreeing with Jesse that she should leave.

"I'm sure," Saralee said, "But I stand by my decision."

They all sat down on the bed.

"We aren't really your parents," Pete said, ripping off the band-aid.

"What? You mean I'm adopted? Why are you telling me this now? What do you mean?" Saralee's mind was whirling.

Of all the things she was expecting, that was not one of them.

"Well, you aren't really, technically, adopted," Leana said, beating more around the bush, trying to find a delicate, easy way to explain the whole situation to her, "You were handed to us."

"We're telling you this because of what's been going on," Pete explained, deciding to answer her third question.

"What do you mean? My parents just handed me to you and you took me with no questions asked? What do you know about what's been going on here? How did you even know about this place? This situation? What's been going on?"

"Mara sent us word about it," Leana said softly, "We used to visit here. Mara was a friend of ours."

"It was a long time ago. Seventeen years ago, actually. We were visiting your parents here," Pete said.

"How did you know them?" Saralee asked, looking between her parents.

"We all went to college together," Leana said.

Pete pushed onward with the story, "Mara, her husband, Felicia, your parents, you and your brother were," Saralee cut him off.

"I have a brother?" she couldn't just let that piece of information slide.

Her entire life she had felt like she had a sibling, that her life was missing something, like she was missing someone. That must have been a sibling, a brother.

"Yes. He was the oldest out of the three of you. He was two, Felicia was one, and you were only a couple months old," Leana was more than happy to talk about the sidequests, it was easier than the rest of it, "His name is, or at least at the time it was, Hunter."

"Hunter?" Jesse exclaimed.

It slipped out before she could stop it.

"Hunter is my brother?" Saralee exclaimed at the same moment.

"Yes," Leana said slowly, "I'm guessing by that reaction that you two have met him?"

"Ya. He saved me. He saved us all," Saralee said.

Pete and Leana looked at each other with a nod. That sounded about right. Even from a young age, Hunter had been a helper, a rescuer. It made sense that that is the reason they knew him.

"Well, we were celebrating Hunter's birthday, when Mara's husband was called away. He was gone for a long time. When he came back, he had been shot. He fell to the ground saying that the town was on fire and being destroyed. We ran out. Your parents had to help save the town, so they handed you and Hunter to us and went to help," Pete continued with the story.

"What happened with Hunter? Why wasn't he with us? Why didn't I know about him?" Saralee blurted out questions without waiting for answers.

"As we were running, he stopped, and I lost my hold of him," Pete said, his head hanging miserably at his failure.

It had been his only job and he had failed miserably. He thought about that failure all the time.

"What about my parents?"

"I don't know about your mother, but your father was killed in the battle," Pete said.

"Her name was Saria. You look a lot like her," Leana said, brushing Saralee's hair out of her face.

"When you were given to us, we were told to change your name if they didn't make it back to get you. We chose the name Saralee, Sara for Saria, and Lee for me," Leana said.

"What's my real name?"

"Janette," Pete said.

"My real name is Janette?" Saralee said slowly, as if chewing it over in her mind, "Why did you wait so long to tell me all of this?"

"At the time it was safer for you not to know. We didn't want you to go looking for them because you could be in great danger by doing so," Pete said, "It was for your own good."

"Wait," Jesse said, "Sorry to interrupt your little family talk, but can I ask, how does Cara fit into this equation?"

"Cara is the only one Mara would trust to take care of Hunter."

Chapter 39

After several hours of conversation, Saralee had escaped from her room and out of the house to think. She had been missing for several hours when Jesse found her. She was sitting on a hill, looking down at a stream. She was so deep in thought that she hadn't even noticed Jesse coming up and sitting down next to her.

"How are you?" Jesse asked as she sat down, pulling her knees up to her chest and holding them tightly.

"Alright," she looked over and forced a smile.

"Hard week?"

"Not so much hard as mind numbing."

"It can be difficult to take in."

"Ya."

"Want to talk about it?"

"It's just so hard to grasp. The people who raised me weren't really my parents. I'm not an only child like I thought. It feels like I've been lied to my whole life."

"To be fair, they did do it to protect you."

"I know, but knowing that doesn't help make it any easier."

"Hang in there, you'll sort it all out eventually, then all of this will be a vague memory," Jesse put her hand on top of Saralee's and gave it a quick squeeze.

"There you two are," Felicia said, coming up to them.

"Hey Felicia, what's up?" Jesse asked, looking over her shoulder at Felicia.

"Mara is looking for you," she said toward Jesse, "Something's come up."

"What?" Jesse asked.

"I don't know, she just sent me to get you."

Jesse stood up and walked to where Mara was waiting for her. As Jesse left, Felicia sat down with her arms behind her back, propping her up and her foot stretched out in front of her. She stared out at the stream.

"Why do you never call Mara mom? It's always Mara?"

"Calling her mom just doesn't seem right," Felicia shrugged, "It never really has."

She had had to grow up too fast the night her father died. After dealing with that, a person isn't a child any longer. It felt too childish to call Mara something like mom, and after everything Felicia had been through, it wasn't something she was comfortable with.

"Do you remember anything about your father?"

"Not really. I do remember that he used to throw me up in the air and catch me. He always smelled of wood. He liked making things out of wood, like a carpenter. Pete was the only one of the men that made it that night. The rest of them died," she said, staring down at the stream, remembering memories she had thought and wished to have forgotten.

Chapter 40

There was something that was worse than death, and Hunter was in it. The torture Flara had in mind had just started, and wouldn't end. She would twist him into her own version of Hunter. By the time she was done with him, no one would know who he was, let alone himself.

Chapter 41

Jordan and James, who had jokingly become known as the JJ's, walked the halls. Over the past few months, they had become good friends. They had spent almost every waking hour with each other.

James had taken on the responsibility of helping guide Jordan into the man he was meant to be. It didn't take too long for Jordan to be given the responsibility of the sword division, and James was there every step of the way to help him.

They had a meeting scheduled, but due to their getting out of training early, they decided to use the break to wander the halls and plan out their course of action. They arrived into the conference room first, taking the seats farthest from the door.

With bows and arrows slung across their backs, Saralee and Felicia burst into the room, their faces red with their exhaustion.

They had spent the morning in the reality course. This course was specifically made to put skills practiced in the training arena, into practical action. They had just finished with a near perfect score, meaning they had managed to find their way through the course with the least amount of casualties or wounded possible. They had beaten their best score. They had even almost beaten Hunter's best score, too. They were glowing with pride at that accomplishment.

Cara and Mara were the last to arrive, with Jesse trailing on their heels. The morning was only halfway over, and already Jesse's mind was ready to explode.

Since she lacked war attack skills, they had decided to use Jesse as a spy, figuring her skills would be better used in the intel game than on the field. Her mornings started early, so as to get as much training as possible in. She had gone straight from her spy training into a meeting with Mara on their defenses and what their plan of attack should be.

"Let's get down to business," Mara said, sitting at the head of the table and setting a folder of papers down on the table, "How are you guys doing?" she asked the JJ's.

"We're doing well. The soldiers respect and trust him and he is doing well when it comes to leading them and fighting alongside them," James complimented.

Cara had taken on the responsibilities of secretary during these meetings, and was frantically scribbling down notes.

"How about you two?" she looked over at Felicia and Saralee.

"We were in the reality course this morning. It went very well. In fact, it's getting better every time we try it. We're in pretty good shape and ready whenever you are," Saralee burst with pride.

"Now that that is out of the way, let's see what else is going on," Mara said, flipping open the folder and looking at the pages, "Flara has gotten five more groups of soldiers of twenty-five men each. There are three archer divisions and two crossbow divisions. They keep in the woods, searching for any signs of our people. The rest of them are either at the fortress or are in their way there now. Also, we need to switch a spy out. He's in hot water and needs to get out ASAP," Mara said, closing the folder.

She took a deep breath to keep herself from sighing and rubbing her eyes in distress.

"We could send a group out to attack her scouting groups, change them out with our own men and have them attack from the inside while we follow and attack from the outside," Jordan jumped in with a plan.

"Or we could let them be. They're going back to the fort, right? So as they do that, we keep them in, make it so no one can get in and no one can get out," Saralee countered.

They brainstormed ideas of what they could do for hours.

"Okay, I'll look through these and we can discuss our move tomorrow," Mara said, standing up with a hold up gesture. She had heard enough, and her head was beginning to pound.

Felicia, Saralee, and the JJ's stood up and walked out of the room, grateful to have a chance to escape and get some much needed rest. Jesse remained seated. Mara had asked her to stay after the meeting so they could discuss a situation privately. She waited nervously while Cara gathered up her notes and she too headed out, leaving Mara and Jesse alone.

"Are you sure you want to do this?" Mara asked, moving over to sit in the seat next to Jesse.

"Yes, I'm sure," she said with a solid nod, "I can do this," she said with conviction.

Her nerves knotted in her stomach, and she wanted to heave up what little she had had to eat that day, but she wouldn't. She had a job to do. She was going to do it.

"It's very dangerous. You could be caught and once that happens, we have no way to get you out. You'll be on your own," Mara cautioned.

"I know. I understand the risks of the situation and I want to do this," she had her mind made up and nothing could sway her from her path, even her frazzled nerves.

"You head out tomorrow morning then," Mara nodded as she stood up.

She placed a hand on Jesse's shoulder for a moment, gave it a squeeze, and left Jesse alone. Jesse took deep breaths as she let her mind sort through her mission.

She had to avoid suspicion while she could sniff out Flara's plans. If at all possible, she would try to locate Hunter and on the even less likely possibility, she would get him back to the portal. If she couldn't manage to get him back to the portal, then she would at least need to get him information on how to get out himself and that help was on the way.

She slowly got up, flipped off the switch and walked out the door, closing the door behind her and headed to her room. She had a tough day ahead of her and she needed to get her rest.

Chapter 42

The room was spinning, even though his head was feeling like it was weighed down with cement and being chipped away at with a jackhammer. All he could manage to do was lay on his back and stare at the stain on the ceiling of his cell.

While it made his head feel slightly better, it left his mind free to wander. Often it chose a most unpleasant path to go down. Every bad memory, every bad thought, was pushed into his consciousness, becoming unbearable to the point of physically causing breathing difficulty. Although the call of unconsciousness was appealing, Hunter knew he was too vulnerable while unconscious. He couldn't allow himself to be off guard.

He fought against the impending darkness for as long as he could, but slowly the pain he was feeling gave way to the darkness, and he slipped into the realm of darkness as the steady thump, thump, scratch of a guard's boots paced up and down the hall of the prison.

Chapter 43

esse tossed and turned, unable to fully fall asleep until moments before she was supposed to be getting up to take on her day. As Felicia shook her awake, Jesse's eyes flew open and she bolted upright in bed.

"What?" she asked, more shocked that she had actually fallen asleep, than she was about being woken up.

"Come on, you need to get up and head out," Felicia said.

Jesse nodded and jumped out of bed.

"Here, this is what you'll wear into Flara's fort," Felicia handed her a hanger of clothes.

Jesse took the hanger from Felicia and hurried to the bathroom that was connected to her room. Before changing into her wardrobe, she threw some cold water on her face, hoping that it would revitalize her and make her look refreshed and not like she hadn't slept in the past 24 hours.

"What do I do once I get to Flara's fort?" she called out to Felicia as she pulled on the costume that was given to her.

"You will walk in and go straight to Flara. If you get stopped, tell them that you have important news for her, that it has to do with Mara's plan of attack," Felicia said, leaning up against the door, waiting for Jesse to come out.

"What news would I give her?"

"Tell her that Mara is planning to surround them and attack full force."

"Will Flara believe that?"

"If she doesn't, then it's your responsibility to make her believe it. Do anything you can to make her believe it."

Jesse came into the room, "No pressure then?" she joked, trying to ease her tension.

Felicia smiled and nodded as she stood up straight. Jesse twirled around, showing Felicia her black riding habit before she threw a cloak over it, hiding it.

"You look great," Felicia said as she took a good look at her.

"Thanks," she said quietly.

"Do you know what you're supposed to do?"

"I need to go in, give Flara Mara's plans, get to Flara's good side, at least enough that she'll trust me, hopefully enough to make me one of her spies. Find Hunter, get him out of prison and to the portal, and stay to get any information that I can without Flara's knowledge."

"Good. Now let's get you something to eat before you head out."

Mara and Cara were already in the dining hall when Felicia and Jesse walked in. Jesse had to do a double take as she walked into the room. Instead of her normal dress or skirt outfit, Mara was wearing jeans and a t-shirt. With her hair in a ponytail, she almost passed as a normal human being.

"Thank you, Felicia," Mara said, rising from the table and coming towards them, "You may go back to bed now," Felicia nodded, and left the room.

Instead of going to bed like ordered, Felicia began to wander the halls. Whenever there was a mission afoot, or she simply couldn't sleep, she would take to wandering the halls. She could slip in and out of any place in that mansion without anyone being any wiser. It was her playground, and she knew it like the back of her hand.

"Come in and have breakfast," Mara put her arm around Jesse's shoulders as Felicia left, "You have a big day ahead of you," she led Jesse toward the table and gently lowered her into a seat.

As Jesse got settled, Mara rang a nearby bell. A plump, cheery-eyed maid came into the dining hall with a bowl of oatmeal and some orange juice on a silver platter. The maid placed it down in front of Jesse with a bright smile.

"Good morning, miss," she said happily, her grandmotherly voice was soothing to Jesse's troubled nerves.

"Good morning," Jesse responded politely.

"Can I get anything else for you? Milk, some eggs, anything at all?"

"No thanks. I think I'm good for now."

"Yes, ma'am," with a curtsey, she left the room.

Jesse picked up her spoon and placed it in her oatmeal. She tried to put some of it in her mouth, but she found she couldn't. Her throat refused to swallow, leaving her with flavorless goop sitting in her mouth with nowhere to go.

"I know you're not hungry dear," Cara said gently, "But you have to eat something."

Jesse nodded and looked back down at her bowl of oatmeal. The sight held little appeal to her. What normally looked amazing, now simply looked like wet chunky cement. Still, she relented. She knew she needed to keep her strength up.

"Scared?" Mara asked.

"Ya, but I'll be okay," Jesse said quietly.

"Of course you will. You've been trained wonderfully. You've done great in training. I have absolute faith that you'll be fine. It's perfectly normal to be scared. Even my best men are scared going in," Mara comforted.

After Jesse had finished what she could of her meal and the dishes were cleared away, Cara took Jesse out to the stables, leaving Mara to go over the notes that were taken yesterday.

The grass was glistening with dew as they stepped into the morning. The sky was a dark purple. The whole world was holding its breath in anticipation of the sun rising. It longed for the tickling fingers of the sun to awaken them, allowing the world to once again come to life, and burn off the dew.

"Good morning, Carl," Cara said as he came into the stables to greet them.

"Morning, Ma'am," he bowed, "Jesse," he said with a smile and a nod in her direction.

She smiled back at him. Ever since their lone conversation in the stables during her first week, the two of them had become great friends. They often spent their free time, what little they had, with each other.

"Do you have the horse saddled and bridled?" Cara asked.

"I do," he nodded and left, coming back with a beautiful glossy, brown horse with a white diamond on its forehead.

His normal rules went out a window when a mission was on the line.

"Diamond," Jesse whispered, almost reverently as she reached out to stroke Diamond's nose.

Diamond was one of her favorites, next to Midnight, that is. She couldn't fathom that she was getting Diamond on her journey. She had anticipated one of the other horses, ones that wouldn't be as deeply missed, like Brownie.

"She's no Midnight," Carl was almost apologetic about it, "But she is a mighty fine horse," he handed Jesse the reins.

"She's perfect," she accepted the reins gladly.

"I'm sorry you can't take Midnight," Carl said, knowing how much she loved Midnight, "But he's our best horse. We need him here."

"It's fine," Jesse consoled, "Really," she placed her hand on his, "Diamond is just as good," she gave his hand a squeeze.

"Good-bye Jesse," Cara gave her a hug.

"Good bye," Carl said, giving her hand a squeeze back, "You're one of the best spies I've ever trained. Good luck," he helped her up onto the horse.

"Thanks," she grabbed his hand once again, "Will you tell the rest of them that I said goodbye?" she looked toward Carl, "And that I love them?" she glanced over at Cara.

This was the hardest part of saying goodbye, not knowing that she'd ever make it back, never knowing if she'd see them again.

"Of course," Cara said with a reassuring smile.

"I'll keep in touch," she smiled at her weak attempt at a joke.

Jesse turned her horse toward the portal and she was on her way.

"You'll do great. Good luck. Goodbye Jesse," was shouted to her as she left Carl and Cara, waving at the stable door.

"Do you want to come in and help me explain this to them?" Cara asked, looking toward Carl.

He had a comforting presence that would make even difficult news easy to hear, she could use that.

"Sure."

They walked to the mansion in silence. Saralee and Jordan were already there, waiting for them. Instead of going on their morning ride, they had been assembled in the library for a conference. They settled into seats and Mara stood up.

"I know this is different," she announced, "But I have something to tell all of you. I decided it would be best if we got this out of the way this morning," she looked around at the expectant faces of her audience. It was so quiet that you could hear a pin drop, "Alright," she took a deep breath, "As you all will recall, Jesse wasn't at breakfast this morning. That was because she wasn't and isn't here."

"What do you mean she isn't here? Where is she?" Jordan asked, anger in his voice.

"She left early this morning," Cara said, "She's headed to Flara's fortress."

"She's what?" Jordan asked.

His heart was thumping in his chest. He couldn't breathe. He couldn't think straight. He was supposed to be taking care of her. The whole point of running away was to get her away from evil people who wanted to harm her, not send her right into their arms.

But most of all, he couldn't believe that she hadn't told him. No one had told him.

"Why?" Saralee asked.

"You remember yesterday? I said that a spy had to be switched out? Well, she's his replacement. She had to leave early in the morning in order to get to Flara's fortress by this evening," Mara said.

"You can't be serious," Jordan said, "She can't be a spy!"

Pressure started to build up inside Jordan. He felt like his head was going to explode. His sister was in Flara's fortress. She was a spy. This couldn't be happening. This couldn't be real. Not his sister. She couldn't do this. They were sending her into a death trap. He couldn't protect her there. They hadn't even let him in on this one. They had kept him completely in the dark until it was too late. He was boiling with fury.

"She asked me to tell all of you that she said gooby and that she loved you," Carl jumped in.

"No, you guys can't be serious. You sent her into a trap!" Jordan jumped out of his seat and started yelling.

"We are serious, but I want you to know that she did this of her own volition. Nobody forced her into it. She wanted to do this," Mara explained gently, trying to keep Jordan calm and under control.

"I do some training with other spies," Carl explained, "I want you to know that she was really good. She'll be just fine out there."

Jordan started to calm down. All of it sounded like Jesse. She was a helper. She would love to help him out in any way she could, and she could act with the best of them. Still, he couldn't imagine that his twin sister wasn't going to be walking in the door at any minute and shouting, 'Surprise!'

He stood up and walked out the door. He needed to release some energy. No one moved as he exited the room.

"So, what do we do now?" Saralee asked, finally breaking the silence.

"Do we do training today?" James asked.

"If you guys choose to do training that is fine with me, but I don't think Jordan will want to, and I'm not going to force him. I won't force you guys, not today. Let it sink in. Tomorrow we'll be back to normal," Mara said and she walked out of the room.

James and Saralee sat numbly next to each other.

Chapter 44

Jesse and Diamond raced through the woods, only slowing as they neared Flara's fortress. Running into Flara's lair would be unwise. She couldn't look panicked, even if that's how she felt

"Hey you! What are you doing here?" Illian asked, his weapon trained on her.

"I have news for Flara," she said calmly.

"About what?"

"About Mara's plans of attack."

He motioned her off her horse. She slipped off the horse and Illian led her to the stables.

"You can leave your horse here," he said.

Reluctantly, she gave the reins to a dark haired, big bodied man who looked like he could crush the fort with his thumb, with hardly any effort at all. He was as unlike Carl as a person could get.

"This woman says she has some information for you," Illian said as he pushed her into Flara's throne room.

"Really?" Flara said with an amused smile, "Please, do tell," she leaned back into her chair.

"Yes, I know what Mara's plan of attack is. She's going to surround the fort and then make a full on attack."

"How do you know about her plans? And why would you give me such valuable information?"

"I overheard them talking about the plans. You see, I'm a maid in Mara's household, so I see and overhear a lot of things. I'm invisible to them. They never notice I'm there, so it's easy for me to pick up information."

"How touching," Flara mocked, "But why would you bring all this to me?"

"I'm trying to care for my aged grandparents, but Mara makes that almost impossible. She raises the costs of everything, but hasn't raised my salary, instead she lowered it, but is making me work four times harder than before and for twice as long, with less payment. She's slowly killing my family and everybody else in the village."

"Oh, so it's revenge. She hurts you, so you hurt her back," Flara nodded, she could understand that.

"Yes ma'am and the only way I could think of to do that, and get out from under her tyrannical rule, is to help you, Flara. You are the one who should be on the throne. You are the one that should be ruling. You can make the world a better place to live. I'm willing to do anything I can to see that that happens," she spoke eloquently.

Flara looked like she was coming around. Jesse might be able to do this yet. She might be able to convince Flara that she was really on her side. She could do this. She tried not to get too excited, she still had a long way to go, but she had made a start.

Chapter 45

Hunter's eyes fluttered, opening slowly only to close tightly again to ward off the light, and all the memories.

'Maybe Flara was right,' Hunter's mind shouted in his head, making him wince with the intensity in which it was said, 'Maybe it was Mara's fault after all. She could have planned all of it; set it up to make Flara look bad.'

He had only been a child. A fairly young child at that. He could have remembered everything a lot differently than things had actually happened. He couldn't believe his memories any more. His whole view had been turned upside down.

"Why do you side with Mara? Why do you protect her?" Flara asked, when he had been taken down to the chamber for his daily ritual of torture, "Does it look like she cares about you? Has she even tried to get you back, sent help? When the portal closed and you were left behind, did you see anyone coming back to help you? Did they come rushing to your aid when the portal reopened? What is she doing that makes you side with her? Did she even try to save your parents? I did. That's why I had one of my men go get her. It was to get her out of harm's way. What did Mara do? She watched as your father died," she stopped her circling around his chair and knelt down next to him.

"So did you," he said through his haze.

"I tried to save your father, but I couldn't get there in time. There's not a day that goes by that I don't regret that I wasn't fast enough. He was already gone by the time I was able to get to him. I know, I know, I should have seen the danger sooner. If I had, maybe I could have saved him. Maybe I could have saved so many others that night. But I was young and naive, and I couldn't see the danger, "What happened after your parents were lost?" she asked, the fake tears quickly drying up.

"You took my mother. What did you do to her?" he was trying to break through the haze, but it kept pulling him back in.

"Once it was safe, I let her go. I had hoped she would make it back to you, but Mara must have gotten to her first. Who knows what she did to her? Now tell me, after you lost your parents, what happened?"

"A lady found me. She took me to Mara."

"What did Mara do then?"

"She talked and then told me to go with Cara that she'd be my new mom."

"Cara works for Mara. Mara gave you to Cara so she could brainwash you while Mara supervised. Mara hated your parents just like she hates me. She'll stop at nothing to bring down the people she hates. She'll tear the world apart if necessary. She's making life miserable for her people."

"How do you know that?"

"One of her own people told me."

"Can I trust you?"

Hunter's resolve was slipping.

"Want proof? The girl's still here. I'll let her tell you."

The door was opened and Jesse walked through it, still wearing her riding habit and cloak. The sight of Hunter's broken body curdled Jesse's stomach. She forced herself not to close her eyes at the sight. She forced herself to take it all in.

Hunter's face was bruised and swollen, making it nearly

impossible to recognize him from his facial features alone. His neck looked unable to hold his head, making his head loll from one side and the other. What was left of his clothing was hanging off of him limply and were filled with grime and dirt. His hair was a wildly growing mass and stubble encased his chin. His once vibrant bright green eyes were dim and glazed over, looking vacant, like all the life had been sucked out of them.

Hunter forced his head to move so that he could look at the girl. His eyes narrowed as he tried to place the girl. He knew she looked familiar, but that's as far as his mind would carry him, even though the answer to his question danced around in his mind. It teased him, coming so close to his grasp, before dancing away again, laughing. It took delight in torturing him.

"Tell him what it's like, living in your world," Flara urged Jesse forward into the room, "He doesn't believe me even though I found him like this, left in the woods by Mara's men," Flara said.

"Well, I'm a simple maid in Mara's castle," she started quietly.

Even saying those words made her feel like a traitor. She felt like she was betraying everybody she had come to care about. She didn't know if she could continue with what Flara was asking her to do. Hunter looked so fragile, so ready to go in whichever direction the wind blew, and right now it looked like Flara's side was winning.

If Jesse continued with her statement, it might completely push Hunter over the edge. It could be the straw that broke the camel's back, so to speak. However, she didn't have a choice. It was either do this, or have Flara find out the truth.

She couldn't do that. She couldn't risk the mission. If Flara found out what she was doing, she'd be locked up and wouldn't be any good to anyone. She had to do this. Right now, it was the lesser of two evils. She could get it all sorted out once she got Hunter back home. They'd find a way to fix everything back in the portal. She took a deep breath and did what Flara asked.

"I'm trying to care for my aged grandparents, but lately that has become almost impossible. She has raised the cost of everything, lowered salaries and makes them work four times as hard and twice as long. It's getting difficult to feed even myself, and pretty much impossible to feed my grandparents. She is slowly killing the town," Jesse heard her voice say.

"Thank you," Flara nodded, "You may go now," Jesse was escorted from the room. After giving her a few minutes head start, Flara called the guards in to take him back to his cell.

"Your excellency, if it would help, I would gladly talk to the poor boy privately and help him get a clearer picture of what it's like in that place," Jesse said, making a low curtsy as Flara came back to her throne room.

"Thank you, but I think we've got him convinced, but I could have other uses for you. Now, why don't you follow Illian upstairs and change out of that dreadful thing you're wearing."

Jesse's stomach dropped. If she couldn't get Hunter alone, how was she going to fix this mess? How was she ever going to get Hunter back? She'd have to figure it out, and soon. Time was running out.

Chapter 46

The setting sun was casting an orange glow on everything that it touched. The stream Jordan was staring at was looking almost golden in the light. He sighed. Jesse would have loved the picture the setting sun on the stream made. The thought caused a stabbing pain to his heart as he realized how much he missed his twin.

"Hey, how are you holding up?" Saralee came up and sat next to him.

"Alright I guess," he said, not even bothering to look over at her, "Under the circumstances," he kept his eyes on the setting sun.

"She's not a child anymore. You don't have to protect her. She can do that well enough on her own," Saralee tried to comfort.

"We were 12 when our parents became monsters. Jesse got the worst of it. I don't know why, but she did. One night, we were sitting in my room. It was right after a brutal night. Jesse was in a lot of pain. I promised her that no matter what, I would protect her, that I would take care of her. I made her a promise to protect her, and now I can't keep that promise," his voice cracked slightly.

He suddenly stopped, clamping his mouth shut. He silently cursed himself. He had lowered his guard and he shouldn't have.

Talking like that made him too vulnerable. People could use that against him, and he couldn't afford for that to happen.

"That was a long time ago. You guys were children. You can't take care of her all the time; she needs to live her own life. She chose to do this; she knows that you can't always be there to protect her. She's not going to hold you to that promise. She knows that that is impossible. You can't protect her where she's at. She's not going to blame you if something happens to her out there. She'll know how much you love her and that you would do anything to protect her," she said.

She gave him a quick, one armed hug and rubbed his shoulders. They sat in silence. There was no need for words, not that there were anymore words to be said anyway.

Chapter 47

Jesse glanced around the room she had been placed in. A twin sized bed was pushed into the right hand corner of the room, but still managed to take up most of the room. The white and black checkered quilt on the bed only seemed to make the room seem smaller than it was. Jesse breathed. It felt like she had gone back to her parents house. She handled it then, and she could handle it now. She had to.

"I'll leave you to change. There are a couple of outfits in the closet. I'll be across the hall, so when you're done," Illian closed the door.

Jesse waited until his footsteps faded off into the distance before heading toward the closet. It was nearly completely bare, only three outfits were taking up space. Jesse ran her fingers along the woolen grey sweatshirt, feeling the softness of the fabric, before her eye fell upon a simple wrap around red dress. Jesse took it out and looked down at herself. This would do.

The fabric of the dress draped about her. A pair of short heels with a flower on the top made the perfect match to the dress. After assessing her look, she nodded and slipped out of her room. Although tempted to snoop around the halls, she knew she was expected back in Flara's throne room as quickly as possible, so she simply made her way across the hall.

"Ready?" Illian asked, stepping out of the room as she approached and closing the door behind him.

"Yes," she nodded.

He took her by the arm and led her back downstairs and into Flara's throne room.

"Ah, there you are," Flara said, as Jesse walked forward.

"Yes ma'am."

"I didn't get your name last time. What is it?"

"Ashleen. Ashleen Carson," Jesse said, picking up the first name that came into her head.

"Well, welcome, Ashleen."

"Thank you ma'am. I'm happy to be here," she curtsied.

"Now, let's get down to business. How long will it be before Mara notices that you're gone?"

"A couple of days, a week at most. A friend of mine is helping me out. She'll do my work for me and will cover for me if necessary, but it can only go on for so long."

"Good. You'll work as a kitchen maid in my household, all the while helping Hunter see the light. Then after that is accomplished, or your week is up, whichever comes first, you will go back to Mara and you will spy on her for me. In two weeks time, you will come back and report to me on anything that you have found out. Deal?"

"Yes, ma'am," she nodded vigorously.

"Why don't you go to Hunter now?"

"Of course, where can I find him?"

Her heart was leaping in her chest. She was going to be taken to Hunter. She'd make this work.

"Blackheart will take you to him, he knows the way."

Blackheart did know the way, because as Jesse was changing, Blackheart had been the one who had taken Hunter into his new room. The new room was just another way to push Hunter over the edge and onto Flara's side.

Chapter 48

Mara took deep breaths, worry twisting in her gut. Her spies always sent updates. They gave her any news they could. Even if they had nothing to report, they at least checked in so that she knew that they were alive. All the other spies had made contact, except Jesse. It had been three days, and no word had come from Jesse.

She had finally reached out to Jesse's contact to ask about her, who in turn had reached out to their contacts, to no avail. No one in Flara's fort seemed to know where she was. A handful of them didn't even know who she was. Jesse had gone dark, not a single contact, to anyone. It was as if Jesse had simply fallen off the face of the planet. She was invisible, lost, vanished into thin air.

Jordan wandered the halls over and over again, trying to keep himself sane. It was driving him crazy not knowing what had happened to his sister. He couldn't sleep, couldn't eat. Even his focus on his new job was lacking. If he only knew that she had made it to Flara's safely, then at least he could relax some, but he hadn't heard from her since the night before she left.

That afternoon, Mara sent for Jordan. As Jesse's brother, he had a right to know what had happened with his sister before anyone else did.

"Where is she? What happened to her?" Jordan burst out as soon as he stepped foot in the room.

"We don't know," Mara answered truthfully, "She hasn't gotten anything to us. Maybe she hasn't gotten any information for us, so she hasn't wanted to make contact yet.

"What about her contact? Shouldn't she have contacted him, let him know who she was or something?"

"It could be that she didn't want to do that before she had information."

"No, Jesse wouldn't do this to us. She wouldn't just walk into Flara's lair and not make contact. She would at least contact her contact. She would let us know she was okay. She wouldn't put us through this."

"Then you may have to face the possibility that Jesse was found out and can't make contact, or that she didn't even make it there," Mara said gently, "We don't know anything for sure, but it is a possibility and I want to make sure that you understand what might happen."

"I do," Jordan nodded, "Perfectly. Every possible situation has gone through my head, over and over again."

"We are not going to give up on her. I will figure out what happened and what's going on and as soon as I know anything, you'll be the first to know."

He simply nodded. There were no more words to be said. His failure overwhelmed everything, leaving no ability to form words.

Chapter 49

Hunter's room was even smaller than Jesse's, if that was at all possible. With a bed inside of it, there was no room to even move around in. It was white and sterile, exactly like a hospital room, giving off the smell of disinfectant and death, exactly like a hospital. Hunter tried not to gag on the stench.

Hunter watched as Jesse sat on the bed, allowing her long black dress drape over the edge of it. For the past three days she had come in and sat with him. She had tried to break the spell that Flara had put over him. Tried telling him of all the good things Mara had done, tried to remind him of his childhood, but it seemed to be of no use. He seemed firmly rooted in Flara's delusion.

Jesse moved closer to Hunter on his bed, and gently brushed back the hair from his face. It was hot and sweaty, his body's attempt to put the pieces of itself back together again. Every breath he took caused him to wince in pain. Jesse's heart pricked with pain as she placed a cool, wet rag on his forehead to try to bring Hunter's fever down.

As she tried to make him more comfortable, she talked to him, softly so as not to be heard by Flara or her men.

"Hey Hunter. It's me, Jesse. Do you remember me? You took us to Mara's world and got caught trying to save us, remember?" every memory became more and more desperate, "It's a beautiful place and

Mara is great. We met Cara too. From what I've pieced together, she raised you...right? So that would make her your mother. Or at least your adopted mother. You're lucky to be from there," it was spoken in more of a whisper so that nobody could overhear her, "I'm going to make you better; at least well enough that you can get back to Mara. She'll know how to help you."

Hunter felt the coolness of the rag hit his hot skin. The coolness felt refreshing after all the heat. It seemed to make things bearable, at least for a moment. As if far away, or underwater, he could hear a girl's voice. The sound was so muffled that words couldn't be made out, but the tone was gentle. It held a comforting lilt to it. It was almost like a mother's voice.

There was a knock on the door and Illian popped his head in saying, "Come on, it's time to leave."

Jesse gave Hunter's face one more pat down before adjusting the rag so it laid on Hunter's forehead.

"Okay Hunter, I have to go," she stood up, "But I'll see you tomorrow," she walked out the door, taking one last look behind her before closing the door behind her.

After three days, Jesse finally had time to make contact with her contact.

Chapter 50

Mara was rubbing her temples in her office when a soldier burst through the doors. Immediately, Mara straightened, ready to receive a report. The soldier handed her a piece of paper and bowed out, letting Mara read it in peace. A smile crossed her lips as she read it. Thankfully she'd have news during their meeting that evening. She got to her feet and hurried to the conference room.

"Alright," Mara said, coming into the room with an open notebook, "Let's get down to business."

"Have you found anything out about Jesse?" Jordan asked immediately.

Every meeting since she had left had started out the exact same way. Mara getting them down to business, and Jordan immediately piping up with a question about his sister.

"I'm getting there," Mara smiled.

"Really? Is she okay?" Jordan asked.

"What did she say?" Carl asked.

He had been allowed into their group meetings when Jesse had left, almost like it was a way to fill the void that Jesse's departure had caused.

Mara picked up the note and started to read.

Sorry you haven't heard from me.
I have been busy.
This is the first time that I had a break since I got here.
I'm safe. Flara seems to trust me.
She's having me work in the kitchens, and work with Hunter.
I'll be back in a couple of days.
I'll explain everything when I get back.

Jesse

"Thank goodness she's safe," Jordan sighed, he breathed easy for the first time in days.

When the meeting came to a close, Saralee headed straight for the hill where she had sat with Jordan the first night Jesse had been gone. A sense of unease curdled her gut.

"Hey, what's wrong?" James asked.

He had seen her walk away from the mansion, a serious look on her face.

"Hi," she said, looking at him, "It's nothing. Something just feels off about this. I can't figure out why."

"Why?"

"I don't know," she shook her head, "It doesn't make sense, but it just feels like something is wrong."

"Well, you know, you can always talk to Mara. Even if you don't understand it, you can explain it to her, maybe others are feeling the same way and she can look into how to fix things."

"Maybe," Saralee said with a shrug.

James placed his arm around Saralee's shoulders, comforting her while she tried to place a finger on why she felt so off.

Chapter 51

Dressed once again in her riding habit, Jesse went to visit Hunter one last time. The swelling around his eye had gone down, so that his eyes were once again visible. The bruising on his body was no longer a deep purple, but a fading yellow and green color, making him look sickly rather than a grape, which had to be better.

Propped up against several pillows, Hunter was sitting up when Jesse walked in the room. He glanced at her curiously. She tickled his memory. He knew her. She had something to do with Mara. That much he knew. He just didn't know how she fit into the equation.

"Hi Hunter," Jesse said happily.

It made her heart soar to see him able to sit up and be conscious.

"Who are you?" he recognized that voice.

Jesse didn't know what to do. This had never been in her training. Change your name so that it couldn't be traced back, yes. What to do when your own person, who may be turned, but not sure of it, asked, never.

"Jesse. My name's Jesse," she had trusted him once, she'd trust him again.

"I know you," Hunter said slowly.

"Yes. You helped me once upon a time."

Visions flashed in his head. The meadow. Men were coming towards them. There were three people. This girl was one of them. They had left him. They hadn't cared if he died. He seethed with anger.

"Get out!" he said, his voice dangerously low, his face full of rage.

"Hunter, what is it?" she startled.

"I said, get out!" he raised his voice slightly.

"Don't do this."

"Leave!" he shouted.

At the sound of the commotion, Illian burst through the door.

"I think you better leave," Illian said.

"I just came to say goodbye."

"Well, you said it, now come on," he took her by the elbow and pulled her out of the room and almost dragged her to the stables.

"What do you want?" the man in the stable asked.

"I need my horse."

"Where are you going?"

"Back to Mara's. Flara is sending me there. Here are my papers," she handed him a note from Flara.

He read it, crumpled it up and went to saddle the horse. It was time for her to go home.

Chapter 52

As soon as Jesse had left the confines of the fortress, Hunter was sent back into the interrogation room.

"Hunter, will you join me in destroying Mara?" Flara asked.

"Yes," he said with conviction, "Anything I can do to help bring her down."

"Good," Flara's face nearly burst with her smile.

"The girl who came in this morning," Hunter started.

"Ashleen?" Flara supplied.

"No, her name is Jesse. She works for Mara."

Flara nodded. She had what she wanted.

Chapter 53

When Jesse got to the entrance of the portal, she slipped off Diamond and chose to walk through the town instead of riding. She allowed herself to soak in the sights. In a few short months this place had become like a home to her.

Jesse was surprised that Carl wasn't in the stables when she got there. At this time of day he was usually feeding the horses. With a shrug, she went to work taking off the saddle and bridle. She was just rubbing Diamond down when Carl finally walked into the stables.

"Jesse?" he asked, stopping short and staring at her with wide eyes of surprise.

"Hi Carl," she walked over to him and gave him a quick, friendly hug.

"What are you doing back? Are you okay? What happened?"

"I'll tell you later, when everybody is together. That way I only have to explain once. Right now, I would like to change."

The mansion was oddly quiet when Carl escorted Jesse inside.

"Training," Carl explained to the curious look on Jesse's face.

Jesse nodded and hurried to her room. She pulled the door open and smiled. It was exactly like she left it. The queen sized bed had a princess canopy over it, giving the illusion of the bed being in it's own private world. The spring time green quilt lit up her room, making it seem bigger than it really was, quite the contrast from the room she had spent the last week in. It was good to be home.

She strode over to her closet and quickly pulled on some blue jeans and a green and white checkered shirt. She let her hair cascaded down her shoulders. Donning flip-flops she decided she was ready to search out her friends. It didn't take long for her to find them. As soon as Carl and Jesse parted ways, Carl had spread the news of her arrival.

She walked into the library and immediately was bombarded with everyone rushing around her, giving hugs and dragging her into the room.

"So what happened? Why are you home?" Saralee asked once they were all situated.

"Well, I went in and told Flara your plans. She ended up taking me on as a kitchen maid, all the while having me try to work on Hunter, trying to break him," Jesse said.

"Wait, why would she have you try to break Hunter?" Jordan asked.

"In order to get her to believe me, I told her a story about how horrible it was here and how cruel Mara was. It was the only way she'd trust me."

"Good job," Mara complemented.

"Anyway, she had me do that for a week, then she sent me back to spy on you guys. I go back in two weeks with what I've learned."

"How is Hunter?" Cara asked anxiously.

"Oh, he looked awful. When I got him he was black and blue from multiple beatings, his face was swollen, and he had several broken ribs. He was delirious most of the time. He had a huge fever and he struggled to breathe. It was horrible to see," she said, her eyes swimming with tears at the memory.

Cara allowed her tears to stream down her face unabated as Jesse continued.

"When I left though, the bruises were vanishing, the swelling had gone down, the fever had broken and he wasn't struggling to breathe, or at least not too badly. In fact, he could sit up for a couple of minutes," Jesse tried to give comfort.

Cara let out a sigh of relief and began wiping at her tears.

"However," Jesse continued, it would do no good to hide anything, they had to know everything that was going on so that they could make this plan work, "He didn't know who I was at first. When he recognized me he started freaking out. He yelled at me. He told me to get out. He put up such a fuss that Illian came in to escort me to the stables."

"You can't go back," Jordan said, as she finished, "Hunter could have betrayed you. It could be a trap."

"No," Jesse shook her head, "He wouldn't do that. He just got nervous when he saw me, that's all. After everything he's been through it was a pretty normal reaction. He wouldn't actually hurt me. He wouldn't betray us like that."

They all prayed that she was right.

Chapter 54

"**W**hen you say working for her," Flara started, "Do you mean, spying?"

"Yes, she talked to me. I couldn't make out the words she was saying, at least for the most part, but I could understand that she had some special connection to Mara."

"Thank you," Flara said sincerely, "Now, why don't you go get some rest?"

Hunter was escorted back to his room and placed in the bed. Flara had already sent some chicken noodle soup and toast up for him to regain his strength. Now that he was on her side, Hunter would be treated with the utmost respect, and was to be taken care of.

In his mind, Hunter went through everything he could recall about what Mara had been planning, the way she thought, everything he could remember about her that he could tell Flara the next morning.

It was his game now.

Chapter 55

That night, after everyone else had gone to bed, Jesse slipped through the heavy oak door of the study. She took a moment to stare at the picture that hung above the fireplace. In it there were three women on chairs, each one holding a young child in their arms. Their faces were bright with laughter as three men sat behind them, resting their hands on the women's shoulders. Tearing her eyes away from the picture she saw Mara sitting at the mahogany desk.

"You'll be leaving in a couple of days?" Mara asked, looking up from the papers that were scattered about her desk.

"Yes," Jesse confirmed, "Flara will be expecting me."

"When you go back, do so with extreme caution. She's cracking down hard on everyone, checking everybody out. It'll be more dangerous going in now than it was the first time around."

"Why? What happened?"

"None of our people know why it's happening or what's going on. My people are trying to figure it out. If we do, we'll let you know, but in the meantime, use caution. If it gets worse, we just won't send you back."

Jesse nodded and walked out the door. She had a sinking feeling that it was Hunter's doing.

Chapter 56

Flara was in a sweat. Jesse would be coming back soon. She had to make sure everything was ready for her return. She sauntered up and down her throne room with her fingers pressed together in front of her chest.

"When you see Jesse, bring her straight to me. Make sure you stay close. I'll be needing you," she explained to Blackheart.

"Yes, ma'am," he said with a nod.

Rickstin walked in as Blackheart left the room.

"Tell your men to stand down when she gets here. We want to make her think that nothing's going on; that everything is normal. I don't want her to be scared away. I have special plans for her."

Jesse was walking into a trap without even realizing. She smiled.

Chapter 57

The dew made the grass sparkle like diamonds in the rising sun. The sky was pastel orange and yellow, a hint of pink graced the edges. Birds chirped happily, as if they had no care in the world. It was a perfect day for idling around, and having no cares in the world.

However, like most days that are perfect for that, that was not to be the case. There was no time to idle, and there were several cares, several worries. Jesse strode to the stables, determination and fear in her step.

Carl was already there. Diamond had already been saddled and was ready to go.

"Morning," Carl smiled.

"Hello," she smiled nervously as she began to stroke Diamond.

"You ready?" he asked.

He knew the answer. An air of nervousness was emanating from her so strongly that it could be felt for miles around. She was scared, and he knew he couldn't blame her.

"Yeah," she nodded unconvincingly, "At least, I'm as ready as I'll ever be," before her resolve could die, she took Diamond's reins and led her out into the early morning.

She had already said her goodbyes at dinner last night. She

wanted to be able to leave early in the morning without having to be bothered with goodbyes. It was better to just get a jump on the day; to get to Flara's fort as soon as possible to see what was going on. Carl helped her get onto her horse.

"Good luck," Carl said, giving her hand a squeeze and the horse a pat.

"Thanks," she returned his squeeze, "Goodbye Carl."

"Be careful," his eyes were filled with worry.

She kicked the horse into a gallop, leaving Carl standing there, watching her ride off, praying that she would be okay, that she would come back to him.

Chapter 58

J esse slowed her horse to a walk as she neared Flara's fort. She got off the horse at the entrance and walked toward the stables with Diamond.

"Wait!" Blackheart called out to her, as she neared the stables.

"Yes?" she jumped at the sudden sound.

Her already rapidly beating, loud heart started beating twice as hard and as loud. She was surprised no one else seemed to be able to hear it.

"Flara wants to see you immediately."

"Okay," Jesse said, "Let me just stable my horse and I'll be right there."

"No," Blackheart shook his head, "She wants to see you as soon as you arrive. I'll have Illian take your horse to the stable. Garon can take her from there," he turned and shouted over his shoulder to where Illian was lolling about, "Illian!"

"Yes sir," Illian hurried to get there.

"Take Ms. Carson's horse to the stables."

"Yes sir," he took the reins and led Diamond to the stables.

Jesse's stomach churned. This didn't feel right. Her heart was thumping loudly in her ears as Blackheart took Jesse by the arm and led her to Flara's throne room.

"Ashleen!" Flara said, rising to her feet as Jesse walked into the middle of the room, "Welcome back. How were things at home?"

"They're okay, thank you," Jesse curtsied as she tried to calm her heart.

Everyone was acting very strangely. There was definitely something weird going on. Jesse tried to figure out what it was, and how she was supposed to get herself out of this mess. Maybe she shouldn't have come back.

"That's good," Flara smiled, "Now, why don't you go up to your room, change and get freshened up? We can talk later."

"Yes ma'am," she bowed and left the room.

Jesse tried to take some calming breaths as she walked to her room, but her heart refused to listen. It stubbornly refused to go back to normal speed, causing Jesse to begin to tremble. After much difficulty she managed to change into the woolen sweatshirt and slack combo. Maybe if she was wearing a sweatshirt, people would mistake any trembling they noticed for being cold, rather than being terrified. Unable to find any other reason to put off the inevitable, Jesse made her way back to Flara's throne room.

It was empty when she arrived. Not knowing what else to do, she glanced down at her shoes, and clasped her hands behind her back. The sound of the door opening caused Jesse's head to jerk up, trying to keep a neutral expression on her face as she saw Hunter tagging along behind Flara.

Much had changed in the two weeks Jesse had seen Hunter last. His body had healed quite a bit. The bruises and cuts were almost all gone. The swelling had completely vanished. In fact, he hardly seemed any worse for wear. However, there was something different about him.

Hunter's face no longer looked like Jesse had remembered. His once wary, but open and kind eyes, now burned with a hatred Jesse hadn't felt since she had left her parents' house. Yet despite the hatred in his eyes, his demeanor showed that of a man filled with hurt.

"What are you doing here?" Flara asked coldly, gone were all the false pleasantries.

"I have some information about Mara for you. You sent me to go get it and bring it back," she said, a hint of confusion in her voice.

She tried to breathe through her fear, but her pounding heart was making even the simple task of breathing a nearly impossible feat. Subtly she wiped the palms of her hands on her slacks, as she pulled the sleeves of her shirt down over her hands.

"Don't lie to me. It'll only get you into trouble. Now, I want the truth!"

"I don't know what you're talking about. I'm telling you the truth."

"Hunter tells me that's not quite true. Now, who are you and what are you doing here?"

"I'm here with information for you. My name is Ashleen Carson," Jesse said.

Even though she was trembling with fear, her voice remained oddly calm.

Flara stood up from her chair and waltzed over to her, "I know that's not true. Your name is Jesse. You have a twin brother, Jordan, isn't it?"

Jesse looked down at her shoes. Her mind racing, trying to find a way out of this situation.

"I'm giving you an opportunity to tell me the truth. Jesse, what are you doing here?"

"I ran away," Jesse blurted out, "I got scared when you asked me my name. I thought you'd send me back, so I chose a name I really liked and I gave it to you."

"Still going to play this game, are we? You had your shot and you blew it," she said in a low, dangerous voice, "Guards! Take her to the dungeon," she ordered.

Blackheart grabbed her, dragging her to the dungeon with pleasure.

Chapter 59

Leana wandered through the halls of the mansion. Over the last 17 years she had tried to put this place out of her mind. Now, after all these years, she had been brought back. She had tried to keep her daughter, her adopted daughter safe, and now all of that was gone. Saralee was now thrown into the middle of a war that had started long before she was born; a war that Leana and Pete had tried to keep her from; a war that had brought her to them. Being here was too much to bear.

Leana tried to remember all the good times they had had. There had been many. She had loved coming here. It was her happy place. There had even been a time when she and Pete had thought about moving to the portal world. They were going to announce their plans that night, but then Mara's husband was killed, and the town destroyed. It was no longer the same. They knew, they could never come back.

She could remember the first day that they had all met. Mara, Saria, and her were all roommates in college. They hit it off, and made sure to stay roommates every year after that. They lived in a haze of ease. It was like living in a dream. The trio had gone out to dinner where they had met three boys. After that, the 6 of them were hardly ever apart.

It was at the end of their senior year when Mara and Saria told the others where they were really from. They told them all about the Portal, and how Saria was heir to the throne, and that Mara was her younger sister. Naturally, the rest of them were curious, and so a trip was planned.

They fell in love with Mara and Saria's world right away. They even had a triple wedding a week later. Leana had never wanted to leave the place, but Pete and she had jobs waiting for them in the outside world. But they couldn't just leave it behind. It drew them like moths to a flame.

Whenever something went wrong in their world, they would simply go to the portal. That night they had gone over to celebrate Hunter's birthday. Mara's husband had heard some commotion outside, so he went to investigate. He was gone for so long, but eventually he ran back inside, only to fall down, dead.

They all ran outside. They tried to get out, but they could get to the exit. They had to stay, to fight, it was their world and they had to protect it. So, Saria handed over her three month old baby and told Leana to go, that as soon as it was all over, they'd come back, but if something had happened they would need to change their name and forget all about the portal.

Saria and her husband never came back. They did what they were told, changed Janette's name, and raised her like their own. They never learned what had happened to Saria. No one but Flara knew what became of Hunter and Saralee's mother.

She never thought that she would someday have to tell Saralee who she really was, or that she would have to go back to the portal again. She had hoped that her life there would be closed behind her, that it would disappear as the wall closed. It was easier to leave the memories in the past when it wasn't staring you in the face all day everyday.

Still, she couldn't completely give it up. Pete had even made sure Saralee did some training, like she would if she had grown up here. In his own little way, he made sure that she had some kind of ties to her past. Leana had also made sure to keep in touch with Mara periodically to let Mara know how her niece was doing, in return, Mara would let them know how Felicia and Hunter were doing.

Now, just like that moth to the flame, she was back. No one could really leave the portal.

Chapter 60

J esse was thrown to the ground of her cell. She looked up just as the cell door was being locked.

'How had they found out? Had Hunter told them? Why would he do that?' all of these questions ran through her head, over and over again.

Without getting to her feet, she made her way to her mattress and collapsed onto it. She was still trying to sort out her thoughts when she felt eyes on her. She tried to ignore it, but the sound of feet shuffling caused her curiosity to win out. Without sitting up, she glanced over toward the door. There was Hunter, staring at her.

"What?" she asked, hurt that he had done this to her, but angry at the same time.

He said nothing. He simply stared at her.

"Why are you doing this? You're betraying Mara and your mother, everybody that you've ever known, to help Flara? She was the one who killed your father!" her voice was filled with frustration, sadness, and confusion.

Again, he said nothing. He simply turned around and walked away. Jesse didn't know what to make of it. What had happened to him? When she met him, he was so strong. He was so ready to fight for what he believed in, to fight for what he thought was right.

He was protective. He would protect the ones he cared about, even strangers he had just met. Now, he was going behind their back and working with Flara, helping her. She couldn't wrap her mind around it. What had Flara done to him? Whatever it was, it must have been terrible for him to do this.

She wished she had some way to get a hold of her contact, to let him know what was going on. She had to pass this news off to Mara. She had to let them know that Hunter had turned and that she had been captured, but she couldn't. She was trapped. There was no way to escape. The sad thing was, she thought, she had walked right into it; had allowed it to happen.

She had told Hunter who she was, when she had no idea whose side he was on. She had come back. She should have seen this coming when she wasn't allowed to take her horse to the stable, she should have ran right then and there. If that wasn't enough of a tip off, Flara's excitement in seeing her should have. She should have run instead of changing, she shouldn't have gone back to the throne room. She had all these signs, and she had ignored all of them.

She had walked right into their trap. She thought she would be fine. She kicked herself for being so clueless, for not using her brain. She had done this all to herself.

Chapter 61

They all gathered in the conference room that evening.

"Flara sent me a note," Mara said.

"What does she want?" Felicia asked.

Mara flipped open the folder and pulled out a piece of paper and read it aloud.

Mara,

I have one of your spies in my custody. If you want to see her again, and save your world from crumbling around you, again, give up now.

Flara.

"We only have one female at Flara's fort," Cara said softly.

"Jesse," Jordan could barely get the word out, "What will she do?"

"I don't know," Mara answered truthfully.

It would do no good to lie to him.

"How was she even found out?" Carl asked.

"Someone must have told her," Mara asked.

"What do we do now?" Leana asked.

This was a far cry from how the portal used to be. The portal used to be a place to run to to escape from problems, not to find them.

"We have to save my sister!" Jordan answered.

"Why don't you two meet?" Cara suggested, "You and Flara can talk, face to face. Find some way to work it out?"

"That could work!" Saralee exclaimed excitedly, "There's a cabin in the woods you can meet at," she thought about the cabin she had been trapped in, it felt like a million years ago.

So it was arranged. A note would be written up and sent to Flara. They would be allowed two people to go with them for safety purposes.

All Flara had to do was accept.

Chapter 62

One of Flara's maids brought in a note on a silver tray. Flara picked it up and waved the maid away. It was from Mara. Flara couldn't keep the smile of success off her face. She opened it and started to read.

So, they wanted to meet did they? She could do that. She'd play their game. Two people were allowed, plus Jesse. She called in Hunter.

"We have a request from Mara."

"Really?" Hunter cocked his head, "What does she want?" he asked, making it sound as if he was as uninterested in what she had to say as possible.

"She wants to meet, at the cabin no less. They want to see Jesse."

"Any other requests?"

"I can bring two people. For security reasons," Flara read.

"Who?"

"You and Blackheart."

"When?"

"We meet at sunrise tomorrow morning. Just be ready to get Jesse out of her room."

Hunter nodded and left the room. Flara smiled. She couldn't wait to see their faces when they saw Hunter standing there, as one of her men.

Chapter 63

Jesse woke up to Hunter fumbling with the door.

"Wake up," he ordered, walking into the cell, "It's time to go."

"Why? Where are we going?" she asked sleepily.

"Don't ask questions, now get up," he bent down and jerked her up by her elbow.

He dragged Jesse to where Blackheart and Flara were waiting. The group marched forward. It was time to meet at the cabin.

Jesse's heart filled with dread.

Chapter 64

Mara, James, and Jordan were walking anxiously up and down the length of the cabin's main room. They were all ready for a fight in case Flara tried to double cross them. The rest of the group was hidden around, ready to go at Mara's signal if needed.

The trio stopped in their tracks as the door was opened and Flara's group stepped in, dragging Jesse behind them.

Her hair was falling out of her hairdo and her face was streaked with dirt. Jordan looked her up and down, trying to assess the damage. She had some cuts, scrapes and bruises, but she didn't look like she had been terribly hurt. Her hands had been tied in front of her body and her eyes were lowered to the floor, and her wrists were slightly chafed from the ropes.

"Ready to surrender to me?" Flara asked.

"You know that's never going to happen," Mara said.

She did a double take as she noticed Hunter standing there, but quickly regained her composure. It was Flara's plan to throw her off, she couldn't let that happen. She'd have to figure it out later.

"Then what is it that you want?"

"I want to sort out some kind of agreement. I want to stop this war before any more blood has to be shed. I also want Hunter and Jesse back."

"You know that is quite impossible. There will be no end until I get what should have been mine in the first place!"

"I know this upsets you," Mara said, trying to remain calm. It wouldn't do to lose her cool, "But it was a long time ago. It was never yours. Just let it go and hand over Hunter and Jesse."

"Never."

Hunter stepped forward, "Why would I want to go with you?" stopping the argument that was about to start, "You are nothing to me, nothing. I never want to see you again."

"What are you talking about?" James asked, stepping forward as well.

His heart twinged. They had been best friends. They had grown up together. They were a team.

"We're on your side," Jordan tried.

"No you aren't. You don't know anything about this. You don't know what they've done. You haven't seen the whole picture," Hunter responded vehemently.

"Then please," Jordan eyerolled, "Enlighten me. Show me the whole picture if you're so smart."

"You don't know anything about Mara, the portal, Flara, me, or anything that's going on. You've been trained to follow orders, not to care about who you're fighting or why. It's all just do as you're told because that's what you've been told to. You only know what Mara has told you or has had you told. Flara has opened my eyes to the truth."

The three of them could only try to keep their mouths from dropping open in shock and disbelief. They couldn't believe that those words had just come out of Hunter's mouth. The damage that was done to him was far worse than any of them had thought.

"Hunter, whatever Flara's told you or made you believe, it isn't true," James tried to plead with his friend, "We care for you. We're your friends. We want to help you."

James' father had died in the same raid that had cost Hunter and Felicia their father's. Always a sickly woman, his mother had gone downhill after that night. She tried to be there for her only child, but she had died a mere three years after his father.

On the day of his mother's funeral, he had met Hunter. They were playing with each other when Cara had found Hunter. After assessing the situation, she had taken him to Mara. He had been taken in by the mansion and there he grew up. He had been an honorary sibling to both Felicia and Hunter. He trained with them, had grown up alongside them.

Over time, he and Hunter felt more like brothers than friends, being inseparable ever since. After everything they had been through together, he couldn't just stand by and watch what was happening to Hunter. He couldn't watch as Flara took complete control of Hunter. He wasn't going to let that happen.

"I think our conversation is over," Flara said, with a triumphant smile over what she had seen Hunter just do.

If she had had any doubts about him before, they were gone now. He truly was one of them. He was hers.

"What about Jesse?" Jordan asked.

"What about her?" Blackheart finally added to the conversation.

"Hand her over," Mara demanded, "She's of no use to you."

"That's where you're wrong," Flara said, taking Jesse by the elbow, "I have plenty of use for her," she dragged Jesse out of the room, "Goodbye Mara. We are going to leave now. If any of you try to stop us or follow us, she will die."

Flara turned, taking Jesse with her and left the cabin with Hunter and Blackheart right behind her.

Chapter 65

Although it was a difficult task, Jesse tried to look behind her as they galloped away. She had no way of knowing when or if she would ever get to see any of them again, and she wanted to take them in for as long as possible.

Sorrow filled her as the cabin was lost in the sea of trees, but she wouldn't let them know that. She wouldn't let them bring her down. That's one thing she had learned at her parents' hand, don't let them bring you down. Don't let them see the pain they've caused. It'll only make it worse.

Chapter 66

Leana, Pete, and Saralee sat in the shade of a maple tree, deep in conversation. Unable to sit still, Felicia paced around the fence of the riding arena, while Cara fiddled with a flower, watching her. Carl had taken himself apart from the group, and was playing with leftover hay. He was the first one to notice the trio making their sluggish way back. He gestured to the others, getting them all ready to greet the group.

"How'd it go?" Saralee inquired as the trio got off their horses and walked toward the stables.

"What happened?" Felicia asked, noticing the look on Mara's face, and knowing that it couldn't be anything good.

"Where's Jesse?" Carl asked, looking around, and simply seeing the three that had left.

Everyone clamored around for details.

"We'll tell you later. Right now, the horses need to be seen to," Mara said and the trio walked the horses to the stable.

It seemed to take forever for them to put the horses away, even with everyone pitching in to help. Once it was all over, they walked back outside. They sat in a circle in the grass, they were too anxious to wait any longer for the details.

"Our plan didn't work out the way we hoped," James said, breaking the silence that seemed to be suffocating them.

"What went wrong?" Saralee inquired.

"Flara is unwilling to let the past go and cooperate with us," Mara explained, "She was unwilling to listen or come up with a way to stop this war before even more people got hurt."

"So, nothing really happened," Felicia chimed in.

She was still confused. They had kind of expected as much. They shouldn't be looking so defeated.

"How can there be people getting hurt when there have been no battles yet?"

"This has been going on ever since you guys were little. Things had been simmering since we were children," Mara explained, "But it all boiled over the night Flara attacked. There have been little battles and skirmishes and anything else Flara could think of to try and make me surrender and leave the portal to her hands."

"Did you see Jesse?" Carl asked, not caring about the history lesson. He had heard it all before.

"Did you get any news about Hunter?" Cara asked at the same time.

"We saw Jesse. She didn't look too badly hurt," Jordan said.

"They brought Hunter with them," James said quietly.

The pain about what he had witnessed still fresh in his mind, still causing pain and distress.

"What?" Leana asked, "Why?"

Granted, the last time she had seen Hunter, he had been a child, but from the updates she received, and the child she remembered, he was a spit-fire. He would be more problems for Flara than he was worth.

"He was one of her two men that she could bring along," Jordan said bitterly.

Hunter had proved Jordan's hypothesis right. It was time for him to find Jesse and get out of there. She was the only person who wouldn't turn on him, the only person he could trust.

"No!" Cara cried.

It was like a knife to her chest. She had raised that child. He couldn't do what they were suggesting. He wouldn't. There was no way.

"You can't be serious," Pete said.

"We're perfectly serious," Mara said, talking more to Cara than the rest of the group, "Hunter has gone to Flara's side. He is now our enemy."

Chapter 67

Hunter guided her down the steps into the prison. Once in the cell he undid her binds.

"What did they do to you?" she asked quietly.

Keeping his eyes on his task, he said, "Flara showed me who Mara and Cara really are; showed me what they're really like. You would be wise to join with us."

"They're your friends. They raised you. They took care of you. How can you do this to them? To all of us?" she asked, hurt evident in her voice.

"They lied to me, just like they lied to you," Hunter had finished untying her hands and looked at her.

"No," she said simply, but with conviction.

"Denying the truth doesn't make it go away or make it any less true. Truth is the truth."

He walked out of the cell, locking it behind him. Jesse stood there, staring at him as he walked away. Her heart hurt for the person she thought she knew, hoping that somewhere deep inside he was still there, and hoping that she could help him find it.

Chapter 68

"We need to be prepared for an attack at any time," Mara said as they walked up to the house.

"Do you think they'll come here?" Leana asked. Her mind raced back to the night they got Saralee.

"They can't, can they?" Saralee asked, glancing at the adults, "I mean, there's magic surrounding it, right?"

"If I know Flara, she'll wait until we are off guard, then she'll send in some of her men to kill as many of us as they can before we find out and they have to retreat. This will go on for as long as it takes for us to start fighting back," Mara said, ignoring Saralee's question.

"Hunter can get through the magic," Felicia whispered to Saralee.

"Can't they rework it?"

"It's not that easy. We're working on it, but it's important that we don't rely on that. We need to get ready for battle," Felicia explained.

Two nights later, they were officially at war with Flara.

Chapter 69

Flara and a portion of her men assembled around the portal, ready to go in as soon as Hunter was able to open it.

"You have your orders," Flara shouted at her men as the wall slowly opened.

They marched into the portal and headed up to the mansion, taking cover in the trees, to make a quick and stealthy attack. As they neared closer to the village, Mara's men seemed to come out of nowhere, popping out from behind trees, jumping on them from behind, and often from above.

James came up behind Illian and raised his sword for an attack. Illian turned on his heels, sword ready. Their swords clashed against each other. James pushed Illian's sword around in a circle before breaking away and coming in for a side attack, but found himself blocked and his sword being pushed up and around. Their swords were just about to break contact when James twisted his sword the other way, causing Illian to drop his weapon. James went in for the kill, but Illian ducked to teh ground, getting the knife in his boot and slashed at James' left leg instead. James' leg gave way, causing him to drop to one knee, his sword laying on the ground.

Flara watched what was going on in front of her. Mara's people were coming in from all sides. Swords clanged against each other.

People were shouting as they fell. Flara's men were dropping around her.

She knew when she was losing, and at this point, she knew that she was, and not Mara that was on the losing side. She also knew that the only thing she could do to keep the rest of her men alive and plan another form of attack was to retreat.

"Fall back! Fall back!" she shouted to her men.

Illian was standing over James when he heard the cry to fall back and go back to the portal. He made one more slash at James, not caring where it landed, and retreated.

Flara looked around at her men once they had cleared the meadow. They were all beaten, sweaty, and tired. None of them had escaped from being cut up and abused on the battlefield. Flara boiled with rage. Mara had won. Flara vowed she was never going to let that happen again. Next time she would be more prepared.

Chapter 70

A young man kneeled down beside James. He was dressed all in black like the rest of the men. His stormy grey eyes stared down at him, his raven black hair, falling in his eyes. He had a bad gash on his cheek, but other than that he looked no worse for wear. He was bent over James, studiously checking out his wounds.

"How many are down?" James asked.

"20 dead, 15 wounded," his voice was rich and silky.

He looked briefly at James before continuing his work.

"That's not bad, not bad," James mumbled, they had been expecting worse.

James' head was feeling fuzzy. The loss of blood was causing his head to spin, and making his world go in and out of focus.

"We're going to take you to the mansion," the young man said, finishing taking care of what he could at the moment, "Hey!" the man waved another young man walking by over to him, "Can you help me take this man up to the mansion?"

"Sure," the man responded, hurrying over.

They carefully lifted James up and headed up the path. There was a tent out back of the tent and went off to alert the doctor and to gather up the rest of the wounded.

On her rounds, Mara noticed James laying on a cot. His left leg looked mummified, all wrapped up in white gauze. Another set of gauze was wrapped around his chest, right below his ribs where Illian had cut him before retreating. James looked groggily up at Mara as she sat next to him.

"How are you feeling?" she asked.

"Like I've been cut by a knife," he said with a twinkle of laughter in his eyes.

She gave him a small smile, "You need to get some rest," she patted him lightly on the shoulder and left the tent.

She had an appointment to make.

"Flara attacked last night. We were able to catch them off guard and were able to gain the upper hand. They didn't have as many men as we anticipated so we forced them to retreat into the forest with only a handful of their original men," Mara updated the others.

"What about us?" Felicia asked.

"We're in good shape. A lot less blood shed than originally anticipated.

"What happens now?" Leana asked.

This wasn't the portal world that she used to know and love. She was used to coming here to escape, not to help figure out wars.

"It was very likely that we'll end up going into a full battle," Mara admitted, "But we'll be ready when that happens."

They'd find a way to win.

Chapter 71

Flara couldn't control her rage. Mara had outwitted her. She stormed down to the prison. Jesse heard the door open and slam. It didn't sound good. Feet were storming down the steps. There was anger in those movements. Someone was furious, and there was nowhere to hide.

Jesse curled up in the corner, trying to be as small as possible so as not to be seen. Hopefully she would be able to escape from the rage that filled that person's steps. Alas, her hope was in vain. With rage like that, nothing was safe.

Flara stormed up to Jesse's cell, keys in hand. She opened it quickly and stormed in. With her dark robes flowing behind her, she looked like a tornado.

"Where are Mara's other spies? What are their names?" Flara asked, rage in her voice.

"I don't know," Jesse said.

She felt oddly calm, even amongst the wrath. Years of dealing with her parents had given her the experience to deal with Flara.

"Don't mess with me. We are ambushed tonight and the information that we were marching tonight could have only come from these walls. Now, I'll ask you one more time. Who and where are Mara's spies?" she jerked Jesse up and took hold of the front of her shirt.

"Why would I know?"

"You're one of them, so you must know something, and from the looks of it, you're pretty big stuff and must be important in the grand scheme of things."

"She sent me to you, knowing that I could get caught and tortured for information at any time. She wouldn't want to put all her spies in danger if one of us is taken. She doesn't tell us who anyone else is. For all I know, I'm on my own here."

"You know something. She wouldn't have asked to see you if you weren't important," she grabbed hold of Jesse's shirt front and shook her.

"Or she could be playing with you," Jesse suggested.

This was nothing new to her. She could handle a raging queen, no problem.

"Fine," Flara seethed, "Who's your contact?"

"Why should I tell you?"

Flara lost her patience. She smacked Jesse across her face and threw her to the ground. She stormed out of the cell and locked it.

On the way back upstairs she told the guard, "She is to have nothing until I say so."

She stormed back upstairs in a fit of rage.

Chapter 72

Jordan woke up before the sun even graced the horizon with its presence. He had a horrible nightmare. He was back at home and his parents had just gotten back home and yelled for Jesse to go to them. His sister wasn't gone long, but when she came back, her whole demeanor had changed.

She looked evil. Her face was twisted into a malevolent smile, despite her cuts and bruises, she looked like she had won something. It was like she had become their parents.

He pulled on some clothes and headed to the hill to clear his head.

'Jesse isn't like that. She wouldn't do that. We're not with our parents. They can't control us anymore. They can't hurt us. They have no control of us anymore,' he thought as he stared out at the dark stream.

One thing he knew for sure, he needed to get his sister back, and he needed to do it now.

Chapter 73

Jesse's breath froze in the air as she curled up on the corner of her mattress. In a futile attempt to keep warm, and help ease her growling stomach, she curled herself up as small as she could. Her chattering teeth just reminded her stomach that it hadn't been fed, causing it to scream in rebellion. She was too focused on her misery that she hadn't noticed when Hunter walked into the cell with handcuffs.

"Get up," he ordered.

"Where am I going?" she asked, trying to keep her teeth from chattering while she talked.

"Downstairs, now get up before I make you."

She got shakily to her feet. Closing her eyes she put her hand against the wall to steady herself as the room spun around her. After giving her a minute to regain some composure, Hunter slapped the handcuffs on and led her down the stairs.

"Thank you, Hunter," Flara said, "That'll be all," she emerged from the dark corner that had been hiding her.

"Now, are you going to be nice on yourself and tell me who your contact is?" she walked around Jesse's chair, "Or do we have to do it the hard way?"

"Never," she said, calmly and quietly.

"The hard way it is," Flara pulled Jesse up by the elbow and dragged her out the door.

"You," she said, pointing at a guard that stood by the door, "Pick a door."

He pointed at the door on the left hand wall. Flara dragged Jesse into the room chosen, the water room. They spent three hours going from room to room, giving Jesse a taste of all the horrors downstairs had to offer. Once Flara was done with Jesse, she dragged a sopping wet Jesse up to her cell.

Jesse could feel the bruises popping up over her body. It made a nice diversion from her throbbing ankle. She winced at the pain, hoping that it was simply a sprain. Her hair had long fallen out of its hold and was now plastered to her head and face. Weak from the day's events, she fell asleep where she had been thrown, with her head on her mattress and arms sprawled out in an attempt to catch herself.

She'd make it through this, somehow, later.

Chapter 74

Felicia walked out to the makeshift hospital after a long morning in the conference room. It felt good to finally get outside, to feel the sun shining down on her.

She opened the tent flap, walked in and looked around at the men lying on cots throughout the tent. Most of them didn't look too bad. In fact, they looked about ready to start fighting again. She walked over to the cot that James occupied. He would be there for awhile.

"I heard you got into some trouble last night," Felicia eyed him.

"Me? Never!" he smiled.

"Oh," Felicia nodded with a smile, "So how do you explain this?" she gestured at him.

"He got lucky," he shrugged, "Now, give me details, what's going on?"

"At the end of the week, we'll march to Flara's."

"I'll be ready," James confirmed.

"Yeah," Felicia shook her head, "I don't think so. You're going to be cooped up in here for a while longer and will have to sit this one out this time."

"I'm fine. I can leave right now," he argued, he tried to lift himself up but fell back in pain.

"I see that," she laughed, "Why don't you get some rest. Maybe you'll be able to help us out next time," she patted his shoulder and left the tent.

It would kill him to be left out, but they couldn't afford to take Mr. Gimpy on this mission with them. He'd be killed for sure.

Chapter 75

Mara's men sneaked into Flara's fort. They took cover in the bushes and the trees. Flara's men were walking about the fort. As they came close, Mara's men jumped out of the bushes and started to attack.

Flara's men jumped into action. They were quick to their feet and weapons. They weren't going to let Mara's men defeat them again. This was their territory and they were going to protect it, whatever the cost may be. They would defeat Mara and victory would finally be theirs.

Felicia was fighting with Rickstin. She jumped from the bushes, sword in one hand, a knife in the other. Rickstin was ready. His sword was already out and he was striking as soon as he saw Felicia standing in front of him. He was trying to work his way up the ladder, he wouldn't allow himself to be bested by a child.

Their swords clashed. Rickstin brought himself closer and grabbed Jesse's other hand in his. He twisted her hand, making her drop her knife to the ground. She pushed him away and brought her sword down to sweep his legs. Seeing his unexpected jump rope, he jumped over it while bringing his sword to her neck, causing her to go down into a squat. As his sword cut the air, Felicia swept his legs just as an arrow hit his chest. He fell to the ground. Felicia turned around and saw Saralee up on a wall, shooting arrows down at the scene before her.

Jordan was fighting Illian. Jordan jumped him from behind, cutting Illian's neck as he did so. Shocked, Illian turned quickly, causing Jordan to fall backwards, losing hold of his knife as his back met the ground. As Illian loomed over him, ready to finish the job, Jordan picked up a fistful of dirt and threw it in Illian's face. As Illian blinked through the pain, Jordan rolled onto his feet, grabbing his knife as he did so.

Mara was in the middle of a circle of three men, all heavily armed. She was fighting one of the men, pushed him away and turned to fight the one behind her. She fought all of them fluidly, but she had been fighting all three of them for a long time and she was slowing down and her fighting was beginning to be more choppy than fluid.

Jordan noticed this and he started to fight his way over to her. Hitting people's swords and making cuts around him, he moved on, not caring what happened to the men he was fighting, just knowing that he needed to get to Mara's side in order to help her. Otherwise, she would be overtaken and Flara would win.

He needed Mara to help Jesse. He couldn't let her die. He jumped into the three on one fight. The swords were blurs that were waving about, never stopping. The swords seemed to be so much a part of them that it was like they had been born with a sword in their hands. They fought so wonderfully it made people think that they had been fighting for their whole life, and that this was what they were born to do.

Saralee moved over on the wall and started firing arrows down at the three men that Jordan and Mara were fighting, trying to help them out, seeing that they were the ones in the most need of some help from above with her arrows. She had just got one of them in the arm when one of Flara's soldiers came up with a sword in hand, ready to fight her.

She was running out of arrows to shoot, and he was too close to make it work. She wasn't able to put another arrow in her bow. She grabbed one of her arrows and ducked down, stabbing the soldier in the leg. She turned upwards, bringing the arrow with her and got him in the chest, watching as he fell off the wall and onto the scene below him, crushing several people as he hit the ground.

Flara could hear the commotion going on outside of her fort. She went out of her throne room, taking all the guards that she could find, with her. She walked out of the fortress, and saw what was going on.

Mara had attacked them, in her own fort. People were fighting all around the open area of her fort. People were screaming in pain and swords were clanging loudly as they crashed against each other. Arrows were flying down from above, almost like it was raining arrows down from the sky. People were running all over.

The soldiers that she had brought with her were already on the field, fighting Mara's men with all their might. Flara smiled as she looked about. It looked like her men had the winning hand this time. It would be Mara, not her that would do the retreating this time. She couldn't contain the happiness that filled her from deep inside of her. She would finally win. She would finally get the victory that she always wanted and she'd accept nothing less.

Mara looked around her as the last of the men who were attacking her had been finished off. Her men were taking a lot of abuse. More soldiers were coming from inside, they were going to be highly outnumbered. Her soldiers weren't going to last for much longer. They needed to get out before they had lost all their men.

"Fall back! Retreat!" she shouted as she headed out of the fort.

Flara could die happy. She saw that Mara's men were falling back, running toward the opening of the fort. Mara was retreating. Flara had won this battle. It caused a well of happiness to spring in her chest. What she had worked for, for so long, was finally beginning. This victory was just the beginning. She'd win so much more. She'd get back what had been denied her parents, what had been denied her. She'd get the portal.

"Victory is ours!" she shouted at her men as Mara's men fled the fort, "We'll finally get what was denied to us!"

The men shouted, their swords raised in the air. They tasted the victory, and once they tasted it, they couldn't stop. They needed more. They wanted to chase Mara's men down and finish them off, which Flara was more than happy to allow.

They cheered and raced after them, leaving a few men to tend to the wounded. Flara floated down to the prison to rub her glory in Jesse's face.

"You guys don't stand a chance, so why don't you help me?" Flara taunted.

"If you think you are so great, and that you are going to win this war, why do you need me? If you're going to win, why should I help you?" Jesse asked weakly, her head was fuzzy and she shook with fever.

"If you help me, I'll remember that when we win. You won't have to suffer like the others will."

"I'd rather die with Mara's men and my friends than betray them in order to escape from it. I wouldn't be able to live with myself if I did that. I wouldn't be able to see my friends suffer and know that I escaped from it because I was a rat and ratted them out."

"You're making a big mistake."

Fara really didn't care, and had no intention of keeping her promise once the war was over.

Chapter 76

Mara's group had barely made it to the portal before Flara's men totally obliterated them. The group was lounging in the library, their adrenaline from the day seeping out of their pores.

"When I was leaving, I heard Flara shout that victory was theirs and that they would finally get what had been denied to them. What does she mean? What was denied to her?" Saralee asked.

"My mom had a sister. An older sister. The sister was always a bit of a rebel, a bit of a 'let me do it on my own,' kind of person, so she ended up running off with a soldier," Mara started.

"Their parents didn't approve and they disowned her?" Saralee guessed.

"So, Flara is your cousin?" Jordan filled in the blanks.

"Yes," Mara said, nodding at Jordan, "Flara is my cousin, but no. It wasn't like that," she turned to Saralee, "My parents didn't really approve, but they didn't really disapprove of it either. He was a soldier and beneath her, but he was a good one, and was pretty high up on the chain of command. They would have been okay with her choice. She wanted something more than okay. She wanted total approval, so she ran away with the soldier. They ended up getting married and not telling anyone about it. My grandparents had no idea that their daughter had gotten married until she appeared with her husband. Well, naturally they were upset, and the match was no longer acceptable. Well, anyway, a couple of months later, my mom married my dad, with the total approval of her parents. So, instead of going to the oldest child ruling when my grandparents died, they put my mom in charge. That filled Flara's mother with rage, she believed it to be her birthright. That rage seeped out and filled Flara as well.

"She felt wronged that her mother didn't become ruler of the portal, and that she in turn didn't get to rule. That anger built up until she decided to take matters into her own hands and she decided to take the portal by force," Mara said, remembering her childhood days.

"That's why she's doing this. She thinks that by right, the portal should be hers, since her mom was the oldest," Cara said.

"That's terrible. I couldn't imagine doing anything like that," Saralee shuddered.

"If you were raised to believe that your aunt was this horrible person and so was the whole family you would end up believing it. It's the way she was raised. That was the mindset that she grew up around. So now she thinks that she's been wrong by her family and she wants to right that wrong, take what she believes should have been hers in the first place," Felicia said.

Saralee almost felt sorry for Flara. She had been raised in a bad situation. It wasn't really her fault, and yet she could have stopped this at any time. She didn't have to go this far, to destroy everything around her, destroy the portal. She didn't have to ruin the lives of all those people. She didn't have to kill Saralee's father, steal her mother and probably kill her as well. Flara had torn her family apart. She had turned her brother against her.

He probably never even knew who she was. Probably never knew that the person he had helped in the cabin was really his sister. She wanted so badly to tell him, but she couldn't. He had fallen into Flara's trap. Now she had lost the brother she had just realized she had, because of Flara. Anger built up within her, as she realized that Flara had taken her entire family away from her without even a moment's hesitation, the sorrow she had felt, dissipated.

Jordan had hoped that he would be able to get his sister out of Flara's grasp during this battle, or at the very least get to see her again, but he hadn't. He hadn't even gotten close to the fortress. He felt like a failure. He never got to see his sister, would probably never see her again. He couldn't even think to be sorry for Flara. He was only filled with rage. He had lost his sister because of this family feud. He had taken her away to escape something like this, and had only run his way into the exact same situation.

Everybody else was too confused to do anything, to think anything. They were tired, upset, and all felt like they were failures. This mission had been a complete bust. Flara had beaten them back. It was going to be a hard night.

Chapter 77

J esse's fever was going down, but her head still felt fuzzy. Nothing around her made much sense. Her stomach growled angrily, it wanted food and it wanted it now. Her lips were parched and cracked to the point of bleeding. Her condition caused the room to spin around her and making her nauseated.

Her mattress seemed to be even more scratchy and uncomfortable then it was before all of this had happened. For the past week she had been down in the chamber for four hours every day. She often wished she could stay down in the chamber all day.

At least down there, it was warm. When she was brought back, it was like a cruel joke. Her room was freezing cold, and her fingers turned into icicles just by setting foot into it. In the chamber, she was able to get away from all that, but in the cell, there was nothing she could do to escape from the bitter cold.

She just wanted to curl up and die, she was so miserable. Her eyes stared unseeing at the wall beside her. With nothing to do and hating the feeling of being so sick, she fell into a fitful, fever ridden dream.

Chapter 78

Flara was getting anxious. Every move she took, Mara seemed to be one step ahead of her. Someone was telling Mara what Flara was up to. She didn't know who it could be. She had only let a few of her trusted soldiers in and told them what she was planning and what was going on.

As she thought, it dawned on her. Hunter! He had to be the one. He was the only new person to be let into the group. She seethed. He had played her game and turned it around to make her look like an idiot. For that, he was going to pay.

Chapter 79

The sound of keys jingling in front of her cell door burst through Jesse's conscience. She glanced up, and through fever glazed eyes, she noticed Hunter standing there.

"Are you okay?" he asked, kneeling down beside her.

"I'm fine," she tried to push herself up onto her elbow.

"Are you well enough to travel?"

"I think so. Why?"

"Come on. I need you to get up," he stood her up and helped her to her feet.

"Where am I going?"

"Home, now hurry up. We don't have a lot of time," he said, hurrying her out of the door.

He quickly locked the cell door behind them and hurried to the cell next to it, ushering the woman on the other side of the door out, before locking that one as well and putting the keys back on the nail by the door. They walked up the stairs and out into the fort. Diamond and another horse were already at the front door, saddled and ready to go.

"Sorry, we don't have time for you to change, but you need to leave. Now. It's not safe for you here," Hunter said.

"It's okay. Why are you doing this?" the woman asked.

"We need to leave," he said again, helping Jesse onto her horse before swinging on behind her.

"Where are you going?" Jesse asked, confused.

"I'm going with you. My job here is done. The big battle is coming, the one that will decide who the winner is and who the loser is. It will decide the person who will rule the portal. It's time for me to be getting home. Now come on," they took off at a run.

Chapter 80

Carl saw figures on horseback, riding quickly up to the mansion. He eyed them until they were close enough to identify. Shock ran through him as he saw Hunter behind Jesse, with a strange lady riding beside them. Of all the things he had been expecting, that hadn't been it.

"Hey Carl," Jesse said weakly as the horse came to a stop.

"Jesse," he smiled, helping her to the ground.

He kept his arm around her waist, stating her need for support to stand upright as an excuse to hold onto her longer than would normally be necessary.

"Hunter," Carl nodded.

"Hi Carl," Hunter hopped off, helping the older woman off the horse.

"Not that I'm not glad to see you," Carl glanced down at Jesse, "But what are you doing here?" Carl glanced up, staring at Hunter.

"I don't know," Jesse said.

The woman remained silent, making Carl wonder if she was in fact, a mute.

"I'll tell you guys later," Hunter walked the horses to the stable and started to take care of them.

Carl kept a wary eye on Hunter the entire time. The woman with them looked shell shocked, and no wonder, it was a strange place to find oneself in. Still, she followed slowly behind the rest as they walked into the conference room.

"Jesse!" Saralee stood up and rushed to her side, giving her the biggest hug she could muster.

"Jesse," Jordan got up and went to her side, "How did you get out?"

They all crowded around Jesse, asking her questions and giving her hugs. Nobody seemed to notice that Hunter was standing with some stranger, right beside Jesse. The group practically pushed her to the table and had her sit down. Hunter, the stranger, and Carl followed quietly behind them.

"How did you get out?" Mara said.

"Hunter got me out," Jesse explained.

"Hunter?" Jordan asked in shock, "Are you sure?"

"Yeah," Jesse nodded.

"But why?" Jordan asked.

"You'll have to ask him."

"How?"

Hunter cleared his throat, alerting them all to his presence.

"Hunter?!" Cara wailed, rushing to his side and wrapping him in an embrace.

Mara's eyes widened in surprise as she glanced their way. Noticing the woman standing beside Hunter, she got to her feet, and in a daze seemed to move toward them.

She may be older, and her raven hair turning gray, and her clothes rags, but she would recognize that face, those eyes anywhere.

"Saria?" Mara breathed.

"Mara," she smiled, her voice held the same musical quality that Mara's did, even though it was still slightly rough from lack of use.

"It is you," they threw themselves into each other's arms, "We thought you had died," Mara pulled away and her hands had taken hold of Saria's shoulders. Tears of joy made her eyes glisten, but they didn't fall.

"It's so good to see you again," Saria responded, "I never thought I'd see you ever again."

Leana stood up and threw herself into Saria's arms as well. The trio was once again reunited, and the held each other fast as the teenagers simply looked around in confusion.

"That's Saria," Pete informed the group.

The words brought the girls back to reality and they released their holds from each other and turned to look at all the kids.

"This is my daughter, Felicia," Mara brought Felicia close to her as she introduced her.

"Saralee," Leana said, looking at her daughter, "Hunter," she glanced over at Hunter, "This is your mother."

Chapter 81

Hunter was gone! Rage filled Flara's soul. She marched down to the prison. She'd make someone pay for his actions, and who better, if Hunter was unavailable, than his little friend?

She flung open Jesse's cell, but it was empty. A pit fell into her stomach. She went to the side, where she had kept her special prisoner, and flung that one open as well. She was gone as well. This was not over.

Her anger built up inside. Someone was going to pay for this. She would crush them all like dirt beneath her feet. She wouldn't rest until she had won. Her vengeance would be sweet. She walked back upstairs and into her throne room.

"How soon will your men be ready to fight?" she asked Blackheart.

"They are willing and able to go as you give the order," he bowed.

"Good. Assemble them and then wait for my signal," she waved him out of the room.

This war had gone on too long. There had been too many delays. Too many games had been played. For too long she had been fighting for what should have been hers. There would be no more stops. No more delays. This was it. She would get back what belonged to her. Tonight.

Chapter 82

The sun had barely made an appearance by the time the sounds of battle echoed across the land. The sounds of battle cries rose to overwhelming heights as the soldiers raced toward each other with the rising sun as a backdrop.

Soldier met soldier with screams and sounds of metal clanging against metal. Shouts and screams rang out as people fell. Arrows fell like rain down onto the scene, not caring who they hit, or which side took the fall.

Amidst the raining arrows, Jordan found himself face to face with a bulky man. His greasy black hair fell into his murderous brown eyes as he attacked Jordan as if Jordan himself was to blame for this war. While his intimidating size was enough to cause Jordan to blanche, it was the man's overwhelming, unshowered smell that really caused Jordan pause. If the man didn't kill him in battle, the man's stench surely would.

As the battle raged on, James found himself once again face to face with Illian. He would make Illian pay for keeping him out of the fray for the past few weeks. With a cut to Illian's arm, Illian dropped his sword, leaving him defenseless to James' attack. Crouching down, Illian scooped up a fallen sword and slashed at James' leg, catching him just below the first cut. As the pain hit him, James fell to the ground, but not before catching Illian on the forearm.

Felicia and Blackheart had found themselves in a sort of stalemate. Their swords were locked in place in an almost arm wrestle fashion. Knowing that her sword would be unable to help her in this situation, Felicia used her free hand to grab the arrows that were on her back. She tried to stab him with her arrow, but Blackheart was too fast. He grabbed hold of her hand, and began to twist it until she had no choice but to let go of the arrow. That move was enough to break them out of their stalemate.

While the rest of their soldiers fought on, Mara and Flara fought their own duel. Somewhere during the fighting they had lost their horses, and were now level as the rest of their soldiers. As their swords clashed together, Mara brought herself closer to Flara and pushed down hard on Flara's sword. Flara and Mara both reached to grab another weapon, but Flara was faster. She brought out a knife, stabbing Mara in the side. Mara let out a groan, but continued to fight, stabbing Flara with one of her arrows.

The day was filled with blood and pain. Determination drove each side, leaving neither party ahead. It was a war that would simply be fought until there was no one left to fight. Slowly, with the sun going down, their energy faded. When they were unable to see in front of their faces, the fighting came to a natural halt. What men were left made their way off the battlefield, ready to fight another day.

Mara walked up to the middle of the field, where her soldiers were gathered.

"All right, listen up! You," she said, pointing to a group of soldiers, "Will be our first watch tonight, then you guys, then you," she said, pointing to two more groups, "Rest up, it'll be another long day tomorrow."

They didn't have to be told twice to get some rest. Most of them were already falling asleep as Mara spoke.

Mara's men were woken up long before the sun had even made

it to the horizon. Flara's men were coming, and they were coming fast. Her men had just enough time to wake up and get to their feet before Flara's men were in the clearing, ready to fight all over again.

Half asleep, Saralee scurried up the nearest tree and started firing her bow and arrows at Flara's charging men. While Saralee scurried for the high ground, Felicia stayed on the same field, shooting arrows at eye level.

As Felicia let her arrows fly, a man came up from behind, putting his arms around her neck as if to twist it. After a momentary fight, Felicia went limp, letting him think that he had gained the upper hand. Once he had settled into a false sense of security, she jammed the arrow she was still holding, into the man's arm.

He yelped in pain, but refused to let go. As she tore the arrow out of her arm, she stomped on his foot, the pain was enough for him to finally release his hold on her. She moved her mouth to the puncture wound and bit down hard. He howled in pain, giving Felicia time to bring out her sword.

It didn't take long before an agile young man found Saralee's hiding spot, and climbed up to meet her. Saralee glanced behind her just in time to see him creeping up on her. With the arrow in her hand, she stabbed him before rolling carefully onto her back. Utilizing her legs, she kicked him in the stomach, which caused him to double over in pain.

He recovered quickly and was soon coming at her again. Once again using her arrow, she knocked his knife out of his hand. It fell until it stuck upright in the ground. Weaponless, he grabbed the arrow from Saralee's hand. As she struggled away from the man, her quill of arrows tumbled down to the ground, making it just as useless as the man's knife. In the midst of her struggle, she tried to get up, but ended up rolling off her tree limb, barely grabbing hold of it to keep herself from tumbling down to the ground.

The man shakily made his way over to her, trying to pry her fingers from the tree limb. Saralee swung herself back and forth in order to get enough momentum to swing herself back onto the limb.

Her sudden movement made him lose his balance and found himself dangling from the opposite tree limb.

Kicking their legs at each other, they tried to make the other lose their hold. A swift kick to the man's chest made Saralee win the kicking contest. Once he fell to the ground, she too released her grip of the tree limb.

As she fell, the man got his knife and swung it at her, barely grazing her arm. Quickly she grabbed her arrows from the ground, and slipped a knife out of her boot. With weapons in hand, they circled around each other. She sliced at him, giving him a cut on a cheek, he grabbed her knife, pulling her close. Unable to get her knife out of his grasp, Saralee grabbed one of her arrows, stabbing him. With him taken care of, she once again resumed firing her arrows into the crowd, trying to help Felicia.

Felicia was in the middle of three soldiers, each one trying to kill her. Years of training had made her light on her feet. Automatically, she skirted away from the blades that were threatening to kill her. A sword came swinging over her, she ducked, slicing the wielder's leg as she went down. Balancing on one leg, she stuck the other one out, causing one of the men to trip. After finishing those two off, she spun back up to her feet and faced the last of the men.

Flara had pushed Mara up against a wall. There was no way for Mara to escape or even gain any ground. She had no footing. She was trapped with no escape. Somewhere during the fighting, she had lost her sword. Flara, however, was standing right in front of her, with a knife in hand, giving Mara no way of retrieving her lost weapon. As Flara brought her knife in for the stab, Mara ducked and tried to get at the knife that was still in her shoe, but was unable to do so before Flara came at her again.

Mara feinted to the left, just as the knife came down. In her crouching position, Mara stuck her foot out and tried to swipe Flara's leg so that she would be able to get her knife and get to her feet in order to gain some kind of footing. Flara easily sidestepped the gesture and continued to stab at Mara.

Jordan had just finished off his opponent, sweat dripping down his face, plastering his hair to his face. He happened to glance over and saw Flara attacking Mara. He could see that Mara would end up dead if she didn't get help. He raced across the battlefield toward them. Using his sword, he distracted anyone who came his way to try and fight him. He came in from behind, but it didn't matter. Flara's eyesight was sharp, and she had been watching his movements from the corner of her eye. She was ready for him. She turned quickly on her heels, slicing him in the side. He cried out in pain, but he couldn't let that stop him. He continued to fight.

Jordan's sword easily managed to knock Flara's knife out of her hand. He moved in for the kill, but Flara managed to duck and rolled away. As she stood, she grabbed a sword that had been lost. Their swords met in mid-air. Jordan pushed Flara's sword in a circle before bringing it down and catching Flara in the leg. As he cut her leg, he was vulnerable, and his arm was cut as well.

Blood seeped out of his wound, sending a searing hot pain up his arm with every movement. He clenched his teeth and fought through the pain. He blocked her at every turn. He got her in the side, right before she swept his other leg, cutting it so deep that it exposed bone. He fell to the ground. In his weakness, Flara had an easy target of his stomach.

Amidst all the fighting, Mara had gotten out her knife, but never had a chance to throw it without the danger of killing Jordan instead. There was no way she could come into that attack with only her little knife without getting herself killed in the process.

As Jordan collapsed even further to the ground, Mara found her chance. The way was clear. It made an easy target. She threw the knife, puncturing Flara's stomach. Flara doubled over and took the knife out as she fell to her knees.

Jordan, still holding his stomach in a pathetic attempt to staunch the bleeding, got to his feet, and stabbed Flara once again. She fell to the ground, dead. It was as if her death held some kind of magic.

The entire battlefield went quiet and they glanced over to see what had just happened.

Flara was lying on the ground with Jordan standing over her, clutching his stomach, sword dangling limply at his side. Mara stood up and walked over to them as Jordan started to way on his feet. Before their eyes, he fell to the ground, seemingly dead.

Chapter 83

Victory was theirs. Flara had finally been defeated. No more would she and her men threaten the portal's borders. Victory was sweet, but it had come with a steep price. Their own men lay beside Flara's on the battlefield, their blood mingling with Flara's men.

After the thrill of the victory had worn off, those that were left standing, took the weapons from Flara's men and tied them up as they went in search for the wounded, which were brought to the makeshift hospital. The people who had survived then made their weary way to their own homes to mourn the loss and revel in the victory.

Chapter 84

Bone weary after working all evening at the hospital, Jesse finally made her way back toward the mansion. Seeing Saralee run toward her, Jesse found a second wind. Her energy levels picked up and she hurried over to meet her. At the sight of the worry on Saralee's face, Jesse's stomach plummeted to the ground.

"What's wrong?" Jesse asked as they met up with each other.

"I think it would be better if you came with me and saw for yourself," Saralee responded instead of truly answering the question.

Saralee led Jesse quickly through the mansion, her jaw set with a determination that matched her stride. Jesse's breath caught in her lungs as they reached Jordan's room. Jesse took a moment to compose herself before she walked into the darkened room.

Felicia had pulled a chair up next to the table in order to tend to Jordan. As they walked into the room, she turned to glance over at the two of them. She nodded at Jesse sadly as she made her way into the room. Felicia automatically relinquished her chair to allow Jesse to take over.

Jesse stared down at Jordan. He was curled up on his side, his blonde hair was plastered to his chalk white face. Each breath seemed to take more out of him than he could afford. Jesse reached out and maternally placed her hand on his burning forehead.

"What happened?" Jesse asked.

"He went to rescue Mara, and Flara cut him up pretty badly," Felicia said.

Felicia winced as she made her way back toward the bed. As she kneeled down beside Jesse, Felicia put a hand on her side, hoping to ease the pain her wound was causing her. Using her available hand, Felicia squeezed Jesse's hand.

"Thank you," Jesse nodded her gratitude for the gesture, but she didn't want to be comforted, not yet, not right now. She just wanted to be with her brother, "Can I be left alone?"

"Of course," Saralee said, giving Jesse's shoulder a quick squeeze, "Come on Felicia," she helped Felicia get to her feet.

As they left the room, Jesse picked up the rag from the nearby basin and started to use it to cool Jordan's fevered skin. Once she was satisfied he was as comfortable as she could make him, she pulled back the covers and lifted the dressings that were covering his wounds.

She was greeted by a long, deep gash that showed some bones on his left side with a stab wound just below it on his stomach. Jesse replaced the dressings, and took both of Jordan's hands in hers. Tears began to stream down her face.

Chances of infection were probable. If the wounds themselves didn't get the best of him, the infection certainly would. She knew all too well that he had days to live.

Chapter 85

"How's Jesse?" Cara asked as Felicia and Saralee made their way into the conference room that night.

"She's doing okay," Felicia expressed, grimacing in pain as she spoke.

"As well as can be expected," Saralee inputted at the same time, "Given the circumstances."

"What happened?" Mara asked, rising to her feet.

Mara's heart started beating rapidly as her eyes began to widen. Her breath was struggling to escape from her lungs. Felicia looked nearly exactly like her father the night he died, with the same expression etched on her face, holding the exact same pose. Mara rushed to her daughter's side. She couldn't lose Felicia. She had already lost a husband, she couldn't lose her daughter too. It was too much to ask.

"I got cut fighting," Felicia breathed, "I'm fine."

"Saralee," Mara ordered, "Take Felicia to the hospital wing to get it looked at."

Saralee nodded and guided Felicia firmly out of the room and toward her own bedroom. Once Felicia was settled, Saralee went in search for a doctor to come take a look at her friend.

By the time the two of them got back, Felicia was lying on her bed, her arms in a circle above her head, cradling it. Felicia moved her head to get a better look at them without having to actually move her body.

The doctor was an average sized man with salt and pepper hair to match. His brown eyes were penetrating and serious. They had long ago lost that youthful zing that they once had. Too much pain had sent that innocence running.

The nurse was much younger, although her green eyes held the look of an old soul. They could pierce through a soul and see all the pain inside a person. It allowed her to be gentle and kind in her treatment, all the while giving a look of understanding of things beyond her scope. She had swooped her hair up into a bun at the top of her head in an attempt to get it out of her hair that caused her to look almost stern.

"Where is it?" the doctor asked.

Judging from his size, the doctor's voice was much deeper than Felicia had expected. Yet, despite the deepness, it held a calm, almost hypnotizing ring to it.

"My side," Felicia said.

She began to lift her shirt and turn so that he could get a better look at it, but fell back

"Here, let me help," the nurse said, her voice, like her eyes, was gentle and kind.

Gently she eased Felicia's shirt up, helping her roll over so the doctor could look at it in the light.

"It's bad, but I've seen worse. You should be fine," the doctor soothed.

As gently as he could, he cleaned the area, put some ointments on it and dressed it. Rummaging through his bag, he produced a bottle of pills. After allowing Felicia one, he set the bottle on the table.

"Give her one as needed," he said, turning toward Saralee.

After a confirmation nod, the doctor and nurse left the room. Saralee turned to her patient, but she was already fast asleep.

Chapter 86

Hunter meandered the hallways, unable to get his mind to stop racing and thinking. With nothing else to do, Hunter decided to check up on Jordan. He slipped into the room. Jordan was still unconscious, not caring who was in the room. Jesse was using one arm to cradle her head while her other clung fast to her brother's head. Hunter smiled sympathetically as he walked into the room and gently shook her.

"Sh," Hunter said softly, "It's just me," he comforted as Jesse jerked awake.

"What do you need?"

"You need to get some rest," he said kneeling down beside her, "In your own bed."

"I'll be okay," she shook her head.

"Jordan will be fine," Hunter assured her, "You can come back tomorrow. There's a nurse right outside, if anything happens before then, you'll be notified," Hunter tried to convince her, "You need your sleep, or you'll be no use to anyone, least of all Jordan."

Jesse glanced between Jordan and Hunter, her decision weighing heavily on her mind. Finally, Hunter's urging won out, and she allowed Hunter to help her to her feet and guide her to her bedroom.

Despite the comfort of her bed, she barely slept. She jumped to

217

her feet and hurried to her brother's side the minute the sun was up. Sometime during the night Jordan's fever had spiked, and he had begun to get listless as he moved his head from side to side.

After placing cool rags upon Jordan's brow, Jesse checked the wounds. The gashes were an angry red, and began to show that an infection had indeed been settling in. With no ointments or any other medicines, she simply placed the dressings back and took her seat next to him.

"Hi Jesse," Sarale eased her way into the room, quietly closing the door behind her.

She had guessed this was where she would find Jesse.

"Hi," Jesse turned around slightly to look at Saralee.

"Have you been here all night?"

Worry creased Saralee's forehead.

"No, Hunter came in last night and made me go to bed. I got up early this morning to take care of him."

"Why don't you go get some air, some breakfast?" Saralee suggested.

"I'm fine," Jesse shook her head.

"You don't have to stay by his bed all day long. It's okay to leave, get some air, stretch your legs. If anything happens you'll be sent for."

"He's my brother and has protected me for my whole life. I can't just leave him now. Not like this," her eyes begged Saralee to understand.

Saralee did understand. Even though she had just met him, she would probably do the same thing for Hunter if their roles were reversed. Saralee gave Jesse's shoulder a squeeze before she walked out of the room.

She made her way down to the training arena and began to jog around it, slipping back into her rhythm almost as easily as she had never left. As she ran she realized how much she had missed it. It had been far too long since she had last gotten to do a full run. Getting tired of running a circle, she ran toward the hill where Felicia was sitting.

"What's wrong?" Felicia asked, she had noticed Saralee's running.

"I'm worried about Jesse," Saralee said, sitting next to Felicia, "She won't leave Jordan's side, which isn't unusual, given the circumstances, but still. She's going to have a rough go of things."

"Well, they are twins, and they have seemed to do almost everything together. It is a difficult situation, but she'll pull through."

"It just worries me," Saralee bit her lip.

"You worry too much," Felicia playfully pushed Saralee.

Or maybe, Felicia didn't worry enough.

Chapter 87

As the days passed, Jordan's health continued to decline. The infection was spreading fast, and nothing had worked to impede it's process. He was living on borrowed time, and any minute he was going to have to give it back.

Hunter had taken to slipping in every night to check in on the twins and would always find Jesse glued to Jordan's side. Hunter wouldn't be surprised if Jesse never moved from that spot ever again.

"How is he?" Hunter asked, looking down at her.

"Not so good," she shook her head, "It's pretty bad. There's nothing we can do," her voice was cracking, "The doctor isn't holding out much hope that he's going to pull through," her eyes were swimming with tears as she looked up at him.

"I'm so sorry," he knelt down beside her, and let her cry into his shirt.

He had felt that pain; the pain that ate away until it had consumed everything in its path. There was nothing for that pain but to feel it. Nothing could be done to ease it. Jesse was going to have to go through it on her own.

Chapter 88

J esse's eyes flew open at the sudden movement of Jordan's hand. With held breath, Jesse stared at her brother. As Jordan's eyes fluttered open, Jesse released her breath and a smile made its way to her lips.

As if taking every ounce of strength he could muster, Jordan raised his hand and pushed back her greasy hair from Jesse's face. She stared at him, refusing to break contact, even to blink. Just as her hair had been moved, Jordan's hand dropped back to the bed, almost as if it had suddenly been made of cement. As his fingers met the mattress, Jordan's eyes once again closed. Seconds later, Jordan's chest fell and refused to move.

For the briefest of seconds time stood still. Silence hung in the air as Jesse watched, hoping to see his chest rise once again. When it remained stubbornly still, Jesse broke down. She threw herself on her brother's dead body and sobbed.

Felicia and Saralee heard a commotion in the room as they walked by the room, heading toward the kitchen, they looked at each other and went inside to investigate.

"Jesse?" Saralee cried out, rushing to Jesse's side.

Felicia immediately went to Jordan's body, checking for a pulse, but unable to find one. Felicia shook her head, answering Saralee's unanswered question.

"No! NO!" Jesse cried, "Jordan."

"Jesse," Felicia said, bringing Jesse into reality for just a moment with the sound of her name, "He's gone," she put both her hands on Jesse's shoulders, "There's nothing we can do. He's dead."

"No," she broke away from Felicia's grasp.

Jesse fell to her knees, her shoulders shaking with sobs. Saralee kneeled down beside Jesse and wrapped her arms around Jesse's shoulders, bringing her close so that Jesse could cry into Saralee's shirt.

"I'll stay with her," Saralee said looking up at Felicia, "Why don't you go tell the others?"

Felicia nodded and walked out the door. She headed to the throne room. She knocked and entered without getting confirmation that she was allowed.

"What is it?" Mara asked absentmindedly.

When nothing was offered, she glanced up from her papers. Noticing the silent tears streaming down her daughter's face, she got to her feet and rushed to Felicia's side.

"What happened?" she asked, more gently.

Felicia couldn't even recall the last time she had cried. Always the strong one, always the one others leaned on for help, she hadn't allowed herself to cry. She had thought the task impossible. Yet here she was, tears falling down her face, surprising even her.

The tears that had spent years not being used, were no refusing to be stopped. They refused to be kept back any longer. They forced their way to freedom.

"Jordan's gone," she said, her voice sounded flat even to her own ears, "He died a few minutes ago."

"I'm so sorry," Mara said, opening her arms and allowing her daughter to grieve.

Like a child, Felicia stepped into her mother's open arms, allowing herself to simply cry, allowed herself to finally be vulnerable enough to be open to comfort. After years, all her sorrows and pains were allowed to be set free. She allowed herself to be the child she hadn't been able to be since the death of her father.

"Cara," Mara called as Felicia's tears subsided, "Jordan died early this morning," she said as Cara entered, "Can you go tell the others? I'd like to check on Jesse."

As Cara made her way to tell the others, Mara helped Felicia to Jordan's room. Saralee looked up as the door opened. Tears were streaming down her face as well. No words needed to be said as the two of them made their way into the room, and together they knelt down beside Jesse and held onto her.

"Why don't you two go and find the doctor," Mara suggested after a few minutes, "I'll stay with Jesse."

The two of them gave Jesse a one sided hug and they left the room. Once they were gone, Mara knelt down beside Jesse and took hold of Jesse's chin. She raised it and turned Jesse's head to face her. Tears were streaming down Jesse's face as she took deep breaths to try and control her sobs.

"Jordan...Jordan," she gasped out, "He, he, he's gone."

Mara took Jesse inot her arms and held her there, "Sh, sh, I know. It's okay. It's alright," she murmured as she stroked Jesse's hair.

"It would be better if she wasn't here," the doctor said, nodding his head in Jesse's direction as he walked into the room.

Keeping her arm around Jesse, Mara helped her to her feet and led her out of the room. Saralee and Felicia followed behind them. By the time the group had reached Jesse's room, Jesse's tears had abated to a slow trickle. She allowed herself to be laid onto her bed without a word. Once on the bed she curled into herself, almost disappearing under the covers.

Chapter 89

As the heavens cried, the group stood around Jordan's casket. The guests had been allowed to drop a handful of dirt into the hole. With each handful, Jesse's air was restricted, as if the dirt was landing in her lungs rather than on the coffin. Jesse stared, dry eyed, as the grave had been refilled. All her tears had been used up, leaving an emptiness that couldn't be filled.

Jesse stayed and watched. The rain grew heavier and heavier until it had driven everyone else inside, and still Jesse stayed. She couldn't gather up the motivation to move. Not even the rain pouring down on her was enough to drive her to her feet.

"Why don't you come inside?" Carl asked.

He had wanted to see her after the funeral, and after being unable to find her in the mansion, he had guessed that she hadn't left Jordan's gravesite.

Jesse stared blankly at him, as if she couldn't understand the words he had just said, and continued to stand, unmoving.

"You're soaking wet," Carl continued, "You're going to get sick if you stay out here."

He placed his arm around her waist and began to lead her toward the mansion. She went without a fuss. She followed as he guided her to her room. While he went to the closet to pick out some dry clothes, Jesse simply stood in the doorway, unable to move.

After picking out some warm, black clothes, he called for the servants to help her get changed. Once they were done, he once again entered and moved Jesse to the desk. She was the perfect model as he combed through her hair. His years of working with horses made him a pro at brushing things. He put her hair in the only updo he knew how to do, a simple braid. It would have to do.

"There you go," he patted her shoulder.

"Thank you Carl," she said quietly.

It was more than she had said in the past week.

"No problem," Carl nodded, "You want to go for a ride?"

She shook her head.

"You know where to find me," he gave her shoulder a squeeze and walked out.

She'd have to come back on her own terms.

Chapter 90

Still feeling weary from grief, Jesse rolled out of bed. Feeling like the walls were beginning to close in on her, she decided to take a walk in the sunshine. Without thinking, she found herself making her way toward the stream. A small smile crossed her lips as she took off her shoes and let her feet play in the cool water as it rushed by.

"Hey," Carl said.

While riding Star, he had noticed a figure standing in the stream. Curious, he made his way over. He was pleasantly surprised to see it was Jesse.

"Hi," she glanced over at him.

"You finally came outside," he got off Star and walked toward her, "Does that mean you're doing better?"

"A little," she confirmed.

It was true. Her heart still hurt, but she felt like she could function a little better now. She was able to enjoy the sun on her face, to feel the cold water on her feet. It was a start.

About The Author

Named after an island in Scotland, Skye Ballantyne's number one thing on her bucket list is to go see the island she was named after. She loves traveling, especially into story settings (via reading/writing) and often finds herself picking up the weird quirks of her characters.

She is also a human's right activist and likes to help bring awareness to different movements through their 'Wear Teal' 'Put a Red X on your hand' days. Except if it requires fake nails, as she has found they incapacitate her and make it impossible to do her work.

Printed in the United States
By Bookmasters